Track Down Wyoming

A Brad Jacobs Thriller

Book 7

SCOTT CONRAD

PUBLISHED BY:
Scott Conrad
Copyright © 2020
All rights reserved.

No part of this publication may be copied, reproduced in any format, by any means, electronic or otherwise, without prior consent from the copyright owner and publisher of this book.

This is a work of fiction. All characters, names, places and events are the product of the author's imagination or are used fictitiously.

Scott Conrad's "A Brad Jacobs Thriller" Series takes retired Force Recon Marine Brad Jacobs and his fellow veterans on dangerous and thrilling international search, rescue and hostage retrieval expeditions. Their missions are to "Track Down" and retrieve innocent victims by facing off against fierce, powerful enemies and extremely challenging conditions.

Enjoy the non-stop action, adventure and mystery with the entire team as they always manage to keep their sense of humor even during the riskiest of operations. Each book is a complete story on its own.

A Brad Jacobs Thriller Series by Scott Conrad:

TRACK DOWN AFRICA – BOOK 1

TRACK DOWN ALASKA – BOOK 2

TRACK DOWN AMAZON – BOOK 3

TRACK DOWN IRAQ – BOOK 4

TRACK DOWN BORNEO – BOOK 5

TRACK DOWN EL SALVADOR – BOOK 6

TRACK DOWN WYOMING – BOOK 7

TRACK DOWN THAILAND – BOOK 8

Visit the author at: ScottConradBooks.com

"Retreat Hell! We're just attacking in another direction."

- Attributed to Major General Oliver P. Smith, USMC, Korea, December 1950.

Table of Contents

PROLOGUE 1

CHAPTER ONE: Day One, 0821 hours 3

CHAPTER TWO: Day One 23

CHAPTER THREE: Day One, 1300 hours 39

CHAPTER FOUR: Day One, 1812 hours 59

CHAPTER FIVE: Day One, 2117 hours 77

CHAPTER SIX: Day Two, 0214 hours 100

CHAPTER SEVEN: Day Two, 0600 hours 116

CHAPTER EIGHT: Day Two, 0637 hours 136

CHAPTER NINE: Day Two, 1604 hours 151

CHAPTER TEN: Day Two, 2117 hours 179

CHAPTER ELEVEN: Day Three, 0109 Hours 200

CHAPTER TWELVE: Day Three, 0100 hours 214

CHAPTER THIRTEEN: Day Three,
0146 hours. 238

CHAPTER FOURTEEN: Day Three,
0228 hours 259

CHAPTER FIFTEEN: Day Three, 0319 hours..... 276

CHAPTER SIXTEEN: Day Three 0230 hours...... 294

CHAPTER SEVENTEEN: Day Three,
0410 hours... 314

CHAPTER EIGHTEEN: Day Three,
0537 hours... 335

CHAPTER NINETEEN: Day Three,
0601 hours... 358

EPILOGUE... 381

PROLOGUE

The old C-130 was on a milk run from San Diego to Sherman Army Airfield at Fort Leavenworth, transporting prisoners for long-term confinement at the U.S. Disciplinary Barracks. The aircraft had made several stops to pick up prisoners from the Corps as well as the other services; the cheap-ass U.S. Government was 'saving money' by using collection points to pick up prisoners rather than flying them commercial (even though the prisoners were being charged for the flight). Harlan Taggart was sick and disgusted, as well as humiliated, by the whole process. Fourteen years in the Corps and this is what he got for fighting for his country, doing what he had been trained to do.

The officers and NCOs that had railroaded him out of the Corps were men he had fought beside, men whose asses he had saved on more than one occasion and in turn had saved his bacon as well. Men he'd thought were his brothers. One little ruckus over some raghead that would probably have gleefully cut their throats and the men he thought of as brothers had turned on him. Bastards! He'd show them! He'd show them all! It was survival of the fittest now, law of the jungle, and Harlan Taggart was a master of that jungle.

The first thing he had to do was get away from this pansy-ass REMF guarding the prisoner detail as soon as the plane made the next stop. They were supposed to get an hour exercise in Denver, and that was as good a place as any to make his escape. Lots of people there, and a couple of the other leathernecks in chains were going to throw in with him. They'd have to kill the guard, but that was his bad luck. No way Harlan Taggart was going to spend the rest of his life in chains, making little rocks out of big ones. No way in hell!

CHAPTER ONE

Day One, 0821 hours

Twenty-three-year-old Nicholas Ainsley, a self-made billionaire tech wizard with a taste for outdoor adventure when he was not brainstorming a new computer application or revolutionary software to sell to the highest government bidder, gazed out over the view from his primitive camp. The land was far more desolate than he had been led to believe, but he didn't care. The outpost store on the north shore of Fayette Lake was a twelve-mile hike away across rugged terrain, but he was below the snow line and the trail was clearly marked. The difference between the Windy River Range and his home in Silicon Valley was astonishing, but he loved the mountains and the fact that the only other people within sight were his friend Simon Perry and his personal assistant, Byron Ashworth.

Simon was his best friend, and together they had hunted elk in Alaska, lion on Safari in Kenya, and bighorn sheep in Colorado. Simon was an outdoorsman in every sense of the word, and he had the skills to back it up.

Byron was another story entirely. Pale, anemic, and whip thin, Byron was a scholarly type who hated the outdoors and was only along on this trip because Ainsley wanted to see how far the guy would go to keep his job. He had been surprised at the dogged intensity of the little guy, staggering under the weight of his pack as they'd hiked in to the campsite without complaint.

He'd actually felt sorry for the guy when he'd seen the mess the hike had made of Byron's feet when they finally got the tents set up and the campfire going. Ainsley had set his tin coffee pot on the fire and the three of them had settled back to enjoy the warmth. The temperature was dropping fast as the sun began to set. Byron tugged off one boot and then his sock. Huge blisters had formed and then popped on his heel and the pads of his feet.

"Jesus Byron, why didn't you say something?" Ainsley got up from his spot near the fire and went over to check out Byron's feet.

"I didn't want you to think I was a wuss, Nick. You and Simon seemed to be doing okay, and I didn't want to hold you up."

Ainsley's opinion of his bookish geek of an assistant went up a couple of notches, though he was appalled that he'd intimidated the young man so much that he'd withheld the fact that his feet had blistered.

"Simon!" he called out. "Bring the first aid kit over here. Byron's been growing blisters and not telling us!"

Simon brought the first aid bag over and knelt next to Ainsley, letting out a low whistle as he surveyed the bottom of Byron's feet.

"We didn't expect you to be a regular mountain man yet, Byron. It took Nick and me years to build up our endurance and toughness, we didn't do it overnight. We are a long way from anywhere right now, so you've got to tell us when something's wrong, man. That could have gotten infected and you could have died out here." He got out a bottle of disinfectant. "This is gonna sting a little, Byron, but I don't feel sorry for you. This is what you get for keeping your mouth shut instead of telling us about your feet." He squirted the spray on the soles of Byron's feet, which really did look atrocious, and winced when Byron yelled.

Ainsley chuckled, not unkindly, at Byron's distress. He wiped the excess spray from the blistered skin and began to slather antibiotic ointment on the tattered soles.

"Going to have to keep these greased up and covered for the next couple of days or they'll get infected, Byron. You'd better take care of them... I have no intention of carrying you out of here on my back!"

* * *

"I think you scared him when you said you wouldn't carry him out of here," Simon snickered. They were on the opposite side of the fire, stowing away the first aid bag.

"I wasn't kidding. I will not carry him out of here, he's going to have to walk out the same way he walked in. There's not going to be any chopper rescue, I didn't even bring a satellite phone. Absolutely *nobody* is going to bother me for the next two weeks, not for any reason. I haven't had a break in three years."

Simon was laughing out loud.

"Poor baby! Works so hard and all he gets for it is billions of dollars! My heart bleeds for you…"

Ainsley grinned at his friend.

"Kiss it, Perry. I *do* work hard for my money…"

"No, you work *smart* for your money, there's a difference. I never said you didn't *earn* it, I said you didn't work *hard* for it. My dad works hard for his money. He sweats and gets dirty and comes home every night dog-ass tired. What we do doesn't qualify as *hard work* in my book."

"I don't have to get dirty to work hard, buddy, and you know it … you're right there with me. I needed this break to clear my mind, we haven't gotten out and away like this in years."

"You got that right. When are we supposed to get our guide?" The State of Wyoming requires non-resident hunters to have a guide or a resident companion.

"We've got to go down to the outpost and meet up with the guy tomorrow. He's going to show us his outfitter's license and then he'll come on out to the campsite a couple of days later. I think, after seeing what the trek out here did to Byron's feet, I'm going to get him to bring along a string of mountain ponies. This country is rougher than I expected, and if we bag an elk I don't think an all-terrain vehicle is going to be able to haul it out."

That had been the plan, having an ATV on call to haul out the carcass; as good a hunter as Simon was (and Ainsley was just as good) there was no guarantee that they'd bag an elk. Ainsley expected to get in some damned fine fly fishing for golden trout in the meantime.

"I guess you're right, but you'd better check with Byron over there." Simon nodded at the assistant, who was lying back on his rucksack, his feet elevated, fast asleep. "Might better ask him if he can ride a horse."

Ainsley chuckled.

"He'll ride a horse all right. I don't think he's going to be doing much walking on this trip."

* * *

This place was supposed to be a paradise, but as far as he was concerned, it was as much a hellhole as anyplace the Corps had ever sent him. It was cold, dry, and he was damned if he'd figured out a way to make enough money to support the team he had managed to put together with the money he and the guys had stolen from that armored car in Denver. The score had been big enough to buy a used fifteen-year-old Suburban in decent shape, and that thing had gotten them to Rawlins, Wyoming before the cops could get organized enough to pursue them. Taggart didn't think he'd left a trail that anyone could follow, but he couldn't be certain.

In Rawlins, Phil Sanders, a former lance corporal and now convicted felon who had been with him when he'd escaped, had contacted one of his brothers who just happened to be a member of a white supremacist group and convinced him to sell them enough arms and ammunition to outfit the eight of them ... the ones who'd escaped the prisoner transport detail at the airport.

Sanders swore that the Wind River Range near Pinedale was the greatest, safest place in the world to hide out undetected. He was so persuasive that Taggart had agreed to take the team up into the mountains until he was certain that the government was no longer actively pursuing them. There was no doubt in his mind that there would be outstanding warrants on all of them, but the truth was after thirty days the most intense pursuit would be over.

Along the way from Rawlins to Pinedale, the group had swelled in number to almost twenty, all sympathetic friends and relatives, veterans of the U.S. military who felt they'd gotten a raw deal after their service. For the most part they had brought their own weapons with them, but Taggart had spent a great deal of the heist money to outfit them with surplus GP Medium tents, mess equipment, and crew-served weapons. The crew-served weapon had come from Aryan Nation in Idaho, and Sanders had mule packed them in himself. Along with him came another dozen veterans, dissatisfied with their lives and brothers in Aryan Nation.

In another month or so, the war chest would be depleted. Small game and fish were abundant in the area, just as Sanders had promised, but staples such as coffee, flour, and salt were only available at the outpost some fifteen miles away ... a trip they could only make on foot. What he had also failed to mention was that it was a cold and unforgiving environment and that firewood was scarce below the snowline. Drinking water was available, but it was a long trek from the stone ruins they were using as a headquarters to the source. Snow was easier to acquire, but it require large amounts of scarce firewood to melt it, and the damned stuff leached minerals from your body.

The ruins were stone-lined round platforms scratched out of the stony mountain inclines, almost at the snowline. They appeared to be the groundworks of wooden structures Taggart thought might have once been lodges. There were stones tumbled about, and Taggart and his men stacked them up as best they could before setting up the GP Medium tents inside the walls.

Taggart knew he would have to come up with a way to replenish the war chest or give up on his dream of establishing real fortress and retreat in failure, a word he'd never believed was in his vocabulary. *Improvise, adapt, overcome.* Those were the words imprinted in him at Parris Island, and he would never forget them... Of course, the

DIs had never expected him to use them the way he intended to now. His tours in Afghanistan had schooled him. *Do what they taught you to do and they kicked you out on your ass. Nobody ever gets ahead by following the rules.*

* * *

"You stay here with the others, Sanders; I'll take Jeffries with me and a couple of the other guys that came with you from Idaho … shouldn't be any wanted posters out on them." He rubbed the thick stubble of his beard. "I'll wear a hat and a pair of sunglasses. That and this damned fuzz should make me hard enough to identify." He heaved an exasperated sigh. "Keep an eye on the guys, Sanders. We're using up staples way too fast, and I can't keep making this trip every week. Thirty miles round trip is kicking my ass and we're running out of cash."

"Gotcha." Sanders was a little awed by Taggart, and he was eager to keep his position as Taggart's

Number Two. Most of the time that was the way Taggart addressed him in front of the others, just like the captain on *Star Trek* or one of those other TV shows always did. It made Sanders feel important.

* * *

The outpost didn't even have a sign outside with a name on it. The wooden structure was built of fir logs, and it looked as if it had stood in place for a hundred years or more. The stony ground around the outpost was worn smooth by the passage of many feet over time, and there was a battered looking vehicle known locally as a 'rock crawler' in a shed outside. Apparently that was how the outpost got resupplied.

The inside was a veritable mother lode of supplies and equipment, everything Nick could imagine might be necessary to survive in such an inhospitable environment, and it wasn't cheap, but that didn't bother him in the least. Nick Ainsley was what the proprietor of the outpost would have described as 'rich as six foot up a bull's ass.'

The guide had not showed up yet, and Nick and Simon entertained themselves by looking at the selection of expensive hunting rifles displayed in a heavily locked case behind the long, worn, hand-hewn slab of wood that served as a counter.

* * *

"Jeffries!" Taggart hissed.

Jeffries, who had been looking wistfully at a men's magazine in a rack full of them, jerked his head up at the summons.

"Huh?"

Taggart waved him over, and Jeffries put the skin mag back in the rack resentfully and moved over.

"Look at those two guys over there! Recognize either of them?" Taggart asked in a low whisper.

Jeffries, a little pissed at having to relinquish his magazine, peered at the two men Taggart had pointed at.

"Sure, the one with the black hair is that computer geek from Silicon Valley. He's in all the magazines an' in the papers. Guy's rich as hell, an' he's always got a hot chick with him wherever he goes. Name's Ansel or somethin' like that."

"Ainsley, Jeffries, the name's Nicholas Ainsley, and he's almost as rich as Warren Buffet or Bill Gates."

"So?"

Taggart shook his head. No wonder Jeffries had never made it out of boot camp. The kid was dumb as a box of rocks.

"Get out of here, and stop looking at him. You wait for me outside somewhere, but make sure you've got a good position so nobody can see you."

"Why?"

"Just do what I tell you, Jeffries, and take the other two with you, quietly... And stop looking at him or I'll put this size twelve right up your ass!"

Jeffries didn't like taking orders from anybody, but Taggart scared the hell out of him ... he was a mean sonofabitch. He gathered up the other three guys from the team and unobtrusively slipped past the ornery looking armed sentry at the front door. The sentry didn't even say goodbye, he was watching the rich guy at the counter.

Taggart moved closer to the counter, inspecting the fly rods on display and listening to the two men talking to the proprietor. Ainsley was doing the talking.

"Yes, we're waiting for our guide to show up. We have to see his license first, we don't want to run afoul of the Fish and Game people..."

"You don't have to worry none 'bout Burl," the proprietor said. "He's been guidin' 'round these parts long as I can remember. Best damned guide in the Range."

"That's good to know, but I still want to see his license and give him the coordinates of our camp."

The proprietor laughed, a deep rumbling laugh that seemed to come from somewhere in the depths of his considerable belly.

"I 'spect he'll be here directly. You don't have to worry 'bout ol' Burl. His grandson is the game warden assigned to your area."

Taggart had heard enough, and a plan was forming in his head as he strolled out past the sentry. Ainsley was going to be the solution to all his problems. It took him only a couple of seconds to figure out where Jeffries and the others were hiding. Thirty seconds later, he was outlining the specifics of his plan. The men were happy. So far, their little soiree in the Wind River Range had been a boring blur of work details. Things were about to get a little more exciting.

* * *

Burl Oates turned out to be a clone of the outpost's proprietor, or vice versa since Burl was obviously the older man. He produced the laminated copy of his guide license and Ainsley pointed out the map coordinates of his camp.

"'Bout where I figgered, fella. Fishin's good up at the lake above ya, caught a four an' a half pound golden trout there last fall."

"Good to know. We'll check it out before if we get a chance before we leave."

"I'll be up there in two days ... got a fella from Denver on a hunt right now, gotta get him his elk ... tomorrow mornin' I 'magine. Elk are movin' good right now in the high meadows, an' that's where I'll be takin' ya."

"Thanks Burl, we'll be looking forward to it." Nick stuck out his hand and Burl shook it. Twenty minutes later, Nick and Simon left the outpost loaded down with food and some antiseptic for Byron, who was resting gratefully back at the camp, and began the long walk back. Neither of them noticed the five men who were following them at a distance.

* * *

The day was gorgeous and the sky was the most beautiful shade of blue Nick could ever remember seeing. The vista was breathtaking, and he and Simon were chatting inconsequentially as they walked, talking about everything but work. The guide was all set to show up, Simon had purchased a bottle of whiskey for them to share around the campfire later, and the prospect of checking out the lake near their camp for golden trout was looking pretty good. Everything was perfect up until a bullet ricocheted off a stone near Nick's left foot.

"Not him, you dumbass! The other guy!"

Stunned, Nick turned around to see a group of men running toward them, one holding what appeared to be an old lever action rifle. An angry looking man with two weeks' growth of heavy beard wearing aviator sunglasses and a fishing hat was yelling out instructions as the group closed rapidly on them. In disbelief, frozen to the ground, Nick watched as the guy with the rifle stopped in midstride and lifted the rifle to his shoulder. He started to scream at Simon, but at that instant, Simon's head disappeared in a spray of blood.

There was no doubt that he could do nothing for his friend, Simon was unquestionably dead ... and the group of men was closing on him fast. Nick dropped his rucksack and fled as fast as his feet would carry him.

CHAPTER TWO

Day One

There is an old saying, "Once a Marine, always a Marine," and Brad Jacobs was the living embodiment of that adage. He had joined the Corps at eighteen, right out of high school. His father had been a career Marine, killed at the end of the Gulf War during Operation Desert Storm while serving under General Norman Schwarzkopf. Brad had always been proud of his father and proud of what the Corps stood for.

A solid six feet two inches tall, he had a muscular build and sandy-blond hair cut high and tight. He had a lantern jaw and a look in his sea-green eyes that said he was ready for anything the world could throw at him, a look that came from an iron core of inner strength. He lived by a code and expected everyone else to do the same.

Brad had spent fifteen years in the Corps, the last ten in Force Recon. When he had gotten out, he had moved back to his hometown of Dallas, Texas, and taken up the profession of bounty hunter, occasionally tracking down and locating missing persons who had vanished while in dangerous countries that traditional law enforcement tended to avoid. From the start, he had always enlisted help from a select pool of friends he trusted, most of whom he had previously served with. Eventually, he'd built a world-class hostage retrieval team (HRT) working for international corporations to retrieve high-level executives who had been abducted in foreign countries.

Mason Ving, his closest friend, had been with him from the beginning. Ving had grown up in a shotgun house in the Central City district of New Orleans, and his mom had died when he was twelve years old. The oldest of three brothers, he had taken a paper route to help his dad put food on the table. The Marine Corps seemed to be his ticket out of oppressive poverty.

A retired Force Recon gunnery sergeant, Ving was a behemoth of a man, six feet tall and two hundred and sixty pounds of muscle, tendon, and bone. He'd acquired a small beer gut since his retirement from the Corps, but it hadn't slowed him down much. His skin was so black that it had blue highlights in the light of day, his bald head positively glistened, and his smiling brown eyes could turn deadly and reptilian when he got riled. Brad learned over the years that when Ving's eyes frosted over it was best to be somewhere else.

* * *

Brad, Ving, and another member of Team Dallas, Jared Smoot (a tall, lanky Texan with a passion for his own blend of hot chocolate ... he carried it with him in a Ziploc bag and referred to it as his 'makin's ... that rivaled Ving's lust for bacon), were on a well-deserved week-long fishing trip for golden trout near Pinedale, Wyoming while contractors put the finishing touches on the barn and the ranch house Brad had bought near Dallas.

* * *

"Hope Pete is havin' fun with that new grandbaby a his," Ving said. He was squatting down by the fire circle he had carefully and lovingly constructed to support the lightweight griddle he had cleverly used as a backboard for his A.L.I.C.E. pack so that he could satisfy his craving for bacon in the wild. Better than a pound of the stuff was sizzling on the griddle while he picked and prodded it with the tip of his Kabar. He had rigged up a travois at the outpost and loaded a heavy ice chest packed with bacon in dry ice along with his pack, rifle, and fly rod onto it. Then he had dragged it the entire distance from the outpost without complaint.

Brad and Jared had liked the travois idea so much that they had lashed together their own, though

Jared had bitterly lamented the outpost's lack of rental horses.

Brad had laughed at him.

"If they'd had any packhorses available we'd have had to haul in feed for them too, Jared. At least this way we only had to bring what *we* needed."

"We coulda brung the Mrazors," Jared grumbled. "This ain't combat ya know."

It was highly unusual for Jared to complain about anything. The lanky Texan was tough as old leather and had endured extremes of combat, temperature, and terrain with a slow smile. Brad wrote off his unusual mood to what he believed was a budding romance with the diminutive Fly Highsmith, Team Dallas's newly hired tech guru. Fly was the first woman Brad had ever known to capture Jared's attention for more than a week or two, and Jared was obviously in the throes of separation anxiety, something he'd never had to suffer before.

Brad and Ving privately believed that the antique sniper rifle, a .52 caliber 1874 Sharps Buffalo rifle in pristine condition that Jared desperately wanted to try out on live game, was the only reason Jared had pried himself away from the ranch ... and Fly. The rifle was a legendary buffalo gun, and a big bull elk would be a real challenge for the black powder metallic cartridge at range.

Brad lifted his fly rod case and threw his tackle bag over his shoulder.

"While you two are lollygagging around the campfire, I'm gonna head out to that lake upslope. The guy at the outpost told me there's golden trout in there, maybe a new state record…"

Jared, busy running a patch down the bore of his Sharps, glanced up at him.

"I'm gonna head out to that long ridgeline back behind us, see if I can zero this thing with this new ammo I got." He didn't trust store-bought ammo; he preferred to load his own. He hadn't had time to pick up reloading supplies for that before the trip, he'd just taken delivery of the rifle from a collector in Dallas the day before they'd left.

"Y'all go 'head an' do whatever ya want, boys, I'm baconatin'!"

Brad shook his head in amusement at Ving's peculiar obsession then turned and began to walk the steep, mile-long incline up to the lake above their campsite.

* * *

The space she had laid out in her sketches was huge, fifty by thirty-four feet. It was larger than her research lab at NSA had been, and there was no bureaucracy to put limitations on her vision. She'd been absolutely correct in her first assessment of

Brad. He was the kind of employer that paid well for expertise, assigned a budget to the task at hand, and then turned the task over to the pro.

She had the knowledge, the expertise, and the necessary contacts in the Intelligence community, and Brad had given her a free hand; he wanted the most advanced communications set-up she was capable of developing. With the seven-figure budget he had given her to work with, she was feeling like a kid cut loose in a toy store with Daddy's credit card.

The contractor's foreman was a competent fellow with a good understanding of what she wanted, and the work was on schedule and under budget, something she had never experienced with a government contractor. He wasn't bad looking either, and another time she might have considered taking him up on his flirting and his offers to take her out to dinner and dancing ... but the foreman didn't hold a candle to Jared. Damn him! Just as she was warming up to him, he ran off for a couple of weeks hunting and fishing with the boys!

Sighing, she turned around and watched as the foreman corrected one of the workmen who had the application of one of the hundreds of coaxial cable compression fittings.

"Dixon! You have to prep the cable end before you put the fitting on, man. Even if it looks clean, make a fresh cut so you're sure the conductor on that RG-6 cable makes a proper connection!"

The foreman turned around and gave Fly an embarrassed look.

"He's a new apprentice..." Shrugging his shoulders, the foreman turned back to watch the young man at work.

Satisfied that the foreman had things well in hand, Fly decided to go over to the big house, where

Vicky and Willona were deciding what colors to paint the rooms. Not such a big deal, but she suddenly felt the need for the company of women. Not just any women but women who knew and understood men like Brad, Ving, Pete ... and Jared.

* * *

The shore of the lake was rocky and barren, and there was snow lying in the cracks and grooves of the stony walls that encompassed the lake. The far shore was flat, though it was stony and rough, all rounded edges as he expected. The water was clear and icy cold, and Brad could see the fish swimming in the water, surprisingly active in water so cold. The fish were a dark reddish gold, with a speckled back much like the rainbow trout he had caught in the Guadalupe River Canyon Tailrace, below the dam.

The wind wasn't bad, and his first cast sent his floating line toward a rock in the water that just tickled the surface of the water, causing a ripple.

The clear monofilament leader with its feather fly attached floated down gently and settled just at the edge of the ripple and was savagely attacked as soon as it touched the water.

The active fish fought energetically, and Brad had his hands full keeping it from throwing the tiny hook. The fight was tense, and it lasted for a good seven or eight minutes before he managed to land the fish.

A shout rang out across the lake and echoed off the rock walls. Startled, Brad scanned the shoreline and finally located a lone man, obviously injured and in considerable pain, trying to run across the rocky ground. There was a pack of men chasing the first one, and that piqued his curiosity.

He carried a compact pair of Steiner 2035 Military-Marine 10 x 50 Porro Prism Binoculars in a stout case packed away in the fanny pack he wore on day trips and hikes, and he quickly dug them out and brought them to bear on the lone runner out in front of the pack. To his astonishment, he recognized the runner, a very public figure, a famous Silicon Valley computer guru reputed to be as wealthy as Warren Buffet or Bill Gates. Ainsley, that was his name. Nicholas Ainsley. His picture was frequently on the front of the celebrity magazines at the checkout lines in the grocery stores. Always had a good looking woman or two hanging from his arms in the pictures. Right now he didn't look as happy as he did on the magazine covers—he looked hurt and he looked scared.

Concerned, Brad shifted his focus to the men chasing Ainsley and instantly recognized the face of the man leading the pack. The beard, hat and sunglasses didn't fool him for a second. There was no way in hell he would ever forget the face of Harlan Taggart, not in a million years. Taggart would be bad news wherever he was at.

There was no question that he had to find some way to intervene. Brad knew he had to help

Ainsley, and, besides, he had a long-standing personal score to settle with Taggart anyway. The drama was unfolding too far away, and at least one of the men was armed. There was nothing he could do but go back to camp and get Ving and Jared. Mentally marking their direction of travel and fixing landmarks in his memory, he raced back toward camp.

Hope I don't trip on one of these rocks and bust my ass! Won't be able to do a damned thing to help anybody if that happens. Why the hell did I leave the satellite phone back at the camp?

The loose stone around the lake bed gave way to grass-covered meadow and Brad picked up his pace.

What the hell is Harlan Taggart doing chasing a multi-billionaire celebrity around the Wind River Mountain Range? Sonofabitch can't be up to any good, that's for damned sure. Hell, I wonder what Taggart is doing out of Leavenworth anyway ... last

I heard they finally caught up with him and court-martialed him down at Pendleton. That was only a few weeks ago, wasn't it? Board found him guilty on all counts, so what's he doing up here?

Got to get back to camp in a hurry! Need to call somebody, but who? FBI? Homeland Security? The State Police? Who the hell would have jurisdiction in a case like this? More importantly, who can I get out here in time to help that poor bastard Ainsley? Taggart looked mad as hell, and unless he has some use for Ainsley, he's going to kill that guy. Wouldn't be the first time, I've known him to do it before for no reason other than just sheer cussedness. Taggart is a waste of good oxygen.

* * *

What the hell? God! They shot Simon! Why?

A stone chip from the first ricochet had clipped his calf like a piece of shrapnel, and Nick could feel the warm, wet blood running down into his boot as he fled. He had no idea why these maniacs were chasing him, but he could see he'd made a serious mistake. Nolan Shepard, his chief of security, had argued like hell against him not bringing a security team up here, but it had seemed an unnecessary precaution to Nick. The Wind River Range was remote and sparsely populated, and Nick and Simon were familiar with the place, they had been here many times since their college days at Cal Tech. The idea of bringing bodyguards (Shepard hated that term, he called his men 'security specialists) had seemed ludicrous.

It wasn't funny now. Simon lay dead a couple of miles back and the only weapon available to Nick was back at the camp ... with Byron for Pete's sake! Byron had the satellite phone; Nick didn't want to be interrupted on his vacation, but the head of a multi-billion-dollar tech conglomerate could never be completely unavailable. Byron's function was supposed to be as a screen, to decide whether whatever was being called about could wait until their return, so the satellite phone had stayed with Byron.

The crazies are too close! If I go back to the camp they'll kill Byron, too, and they're so close behind I'll never get to my rifle in time. Think, Ainsley!

He formulated a plan as he ran. The only chance he had was to find a way to elude his pursuers. Find a place to hide and then circle back to the camp under cover of darkness so he could arm himself and use the satellite phone to call for help. It wasn't much of a plan, but it was all he could come up with at the moment. He didn't figure in the injury to his leg, though, and he didn't realize just how much blood he had lost...

CHAPTER THREE

Day One, 1300 hours

The camp was in sight, and Ving was still "baconating". Ving glanced up from his mostly empty griddle as he stuffed two more crisp pieces of bacon in his mouth. Jared was nowhere to be seen.

"Saddle up, Ving! Trouble!" Brad shouted as he dove for the door of his lightweight mountain tent.

Ving had known Brad for many years, and he recognized the urgency in Brad's voice. Leaving his prized griddle with bacon still sizzling on it lying on the ground beside the makeshift stove, he reached inside his own tent, scarfed up the butt pack he'd prepared for day trips, and then grabbed the Remington Model 700 SPS Tactical in .308 and the single box of cartridges he'd brought along. He had no idea what was up, but there was no question in his mind. When Brad's voice carried that tone, there was probably shooting business at hand.

"Ever heard of Nicholas Ainsley?" Brad shouted from his tent.

Ving heard the nine-lug bolt on Brad's Weatherby Mark V rack open and shut, and the possibility of 'shooting business' transitioned from *probably* to *certainly* in his mind. He loaded the magazine in the Remington with four cartridges and emptied the rest of the box into his vest pockets. Then he checked the spare magazine pouch on his belt to see if the mags for his Glock 17 were fully charged. All three of them open-carried sidearms when they hunted as a matter of course; they would have felt foolish and naked without them.

"I think so... He's that rich computer geek always has his picture on the front a Willona's magazines, right?"

"Yeah. He's out there across the lake and he's being chased by five guys. Looks like he's hurt and at least one of the pursuers has a rifle."

"So I'm guessin' we gonna go after him?"

"We are."

"I ain't against mixin' it up with some bad guys, Brad, but why don't we jist call the game warden or the state cops an' let them handle it? I got bacon cookin' here ya know…"

"You remember Harlan Taggart?"

"Oh hell yeah!" Ving didn't believe in carrying around hate inside, it was too draining. Life was too short to waste it on hating folks, there was more important stuff to do… But for Harlan Taggart he could make an exception.

"He was leading the pack that was chasing Ainsley…"

Ving was on his feet and out the door of the tent in an instant.

"Which way they headed?" he asked, bending over and snatching up the bacon left on the griddle. He blotted the grease off with a paper towel while Brad was backing out of his tent, sat phone in one hand and pen and pad in the other.

"Eat your bacon, Ving, I've got to leave a note for Jared and then give Fly a call."

"Fly? What can she do? We din't bring none a her fancy gizmos with us, Brad, this was s'posed to be a relaxin' huntin' trip..."

"We don't have time to figure out whose jurisdiction this will fall under, Ving, we don't even have time to wait for Jared. We've got to get after that bunch of cutthroats before they catch Ainsley. You know what Taggart's like. Fly can figure out who's got jurisdiction, and she'll know how to find out who has the closest available personnel and resources ... get us some help out here in a hurry."

"How many a them gomers you say was with Taggart?"

"I counted five guys, including Taggart..."

Ving laughed. "Only five?"

"We can probably take him, Ving, especially after Jared catches up to us."

"Yeah, that man can flat fly in the boonies when he's trackin'."

Brad had known some of the best trackers in Force Recon, meaning some of the best in the world, but none of them could hold a candle to Jared Smoot. He had seen Jared trail a single Al-Qaeda assassin across the trackless wastes of Al-Ḥajarah, the western part of Iraq's southern desert. The Iraqi desert has a complex topography of rocky desert, wadis, ridges, and depressions, and even with current technologies, tracking a single individual is virtually impossible ... except for Jared. His instincts worked when technology would not.

Harlan Taggart was a stone killer, and that was a fact, but the chasing scenario didn't make sense to Ving. In fact, nothing about this made any sense.

"You sure it was Taggart? I thought I read in the paper he was court-martialed out in San Diego 'bout a month ago."

"He was, and he was sentenced to life ... in Leavenworth."

"Then whut's he doin' in Wyomin'?" Ving chewed on his bacon thoughtfully, his butt pack in place and his rifle resting in the crooks of his arms.

"Had to have gotten loose during transport from Diego to Leavenworth, I'll have Fly check on it," Brad grunted as he checked his own ammo. He had two boxes of the .300 Weatherby magnum cartridges and a box of match grade .45 ammo for the M45 MEUSOC he carried on his hip. The pistol had been accurized and given to him on his separation from the Corps and he had a sentimental attachment to it.

"If he did, he musta had one a them civilian contractor types watchin' him during transport." Ving chewed furiously on the wad of bacon in his mouth. He already hated Harlan Taggart; having to eat his bacon without getting a chance to enjoy the experience was seriously pissing him off. Sacrilege!

Brad didn't respond, he already had the satellite phone wedged between his chin and his shoulder, his right hand scribbling furiously on the notebook he had resting on his knee. He was speaking into the phone in a low voice, and Ving couldn't make out what he was saying, even though he was only about fifteen feet away. That didn't matter. Ving's juices were flowing and his body was gearing up for combat. Brad punched the "end" button and tore the page he had been scribbling on out of the small notebook, affixing the page to the flap on the front of Jared's tent.

"Let's move out, Ving!" Brad was moving fast and he didn't bother to look and see if Ving was following, he didn't have to.

* * *

Fly heard the disconnect tone and refastened the satellite phone to the hook on the belt she wore around her waist. The guys referred to it as her "Utility Belt" in a teasing reference to the one worn by the cartoon character *Batman* because of all the tech gadgets she kept there. She had to get to Vicky right away. How the hell Brad Jacobs could turn a fishing and hunting vacation with the boys in the middle of nowhere, godforsaken Nowhere, Wyoming, into a damned Federal case was beyond her. It was a little frustrating because she was so busy with the Comm Room project, but it was exciting and a little frightening too.

Nicholas Ainsley was a big deal, no doubt about that. The guy was a serious tech celebrity and so recognizable that even non techies recognized him. He was rich as Croesus, and that made him famous even to people who didn't know a byte from a bite. He was positively gorgeous to boot, and every chippie on the West Coast threw herself at him. He collected starlets and models the way raw meat drew flies.

She ran down an internal list as she raced for the big house, all the agencies who would have jurisdiction on a case like this. This was going to be tough because even though *she* trusted Brad and believed in him implicitly, the F.B.I., who generally handled kidnappings (Ainsley had money and that *had* to be the reason some maniac was chasing him around Wyoming), would be reluctant to start an investigation without a formal complaint … and Fly had no *standing*. She had no personal knowledge other than Brad's phone call that a crime had in fact been committed.

She would have to call Ainsley's headquarters in Silicon Valley to see if she could get someone there to request an investigation, but her experience with tech companies in California told her that she would be viewed and treated as just another attention-seeking crackpot trying to hook up with Nick Ainsley. She was going to have to call in some favors with one or more of the agencies ... but who?

* * *

Nick led them on a merry chase; he knew the area better even than he had let on to Burl, and he was in excellent physical condition despite the fact that he worked behind a desk eight to ten hours a day. He was a jogger, running every morning before work, and he had a fitness center in the office for his employees filled with high-end gym equipment. He and Simon had set the example for the employees, working out daily and providing paid exercise time for them because they believed that the ability to think clearly was dependent on the maintenance of a healthy body.

He had not, however, figured on the debilitation brought on by blood loss. Even so, Taggart didn't catch him until well after dark, and by then they were several miles north of the site where Byron was camped.

* * *

"Gotcha, you sonofabitch!" Jeffries screamed as he grabbed Ainsley and slammed him to the ground. Ainsley had been hiding in a crevice between two boulders at the bottom of a dry wash, a good place of concealment had it not been for the growing blood trail Ainsley was leaving behind.

Taggart reached them only a second later and slapped Jeffries across the back, making a loud sound but not really hurting the man.

"Jeffries! That ain't no way to be treatin' our guest!" He reached down and offered Ainsley his hand, helping him to his feet. Ainsley was exhausted and he was dizzy. "Mr. Ainsley here, he ain't done nothin' to you, Jeffries; tell the man you're sorry..."

Jeffries gave Taggart a resentful glare, but he was wise enough to play along. He had no idea what Taggart was up to, but he knew damned well it was not safe to cross him.

"I'm ... sorry," he said with a total lack of sincerity.

"I'm sorry, *Mr. Ainsley,*" Taggart growled. Jeffries dared a short glance at Taggart and saw the warning signs in the man's hazel eyes.

"I'm sorry, Mr. Ainsley," Jeffries said quietly. He carefully backed out of Taggart's reach before taking his canteen from its case and taking a drink from it.

Ainsley looked at his captor curiously. His behavior did not match up with the angry-sounding lunatic who had killed Simon and chased him across the rocky wastes mercilessly all afternoon. The jerk who had slammed him to the ground certainly did, but this guy, apparently the leader, seemed different.

Taggart took his own canteen out and unscrewed the top then proffered it to Ainsley.

"Here, take a sip of this, it'll be good for what ails you. I warn you, though, it ain't water…"

Ainsley took the canteen then sniffed the contents suspiciously. Bourbon … good bourbon from the smell of it. He wanted water, his body cried out for it, but his gut told him this man would take his refusal to drink from the canteen as an insult. He stuck his tongue on the mouth of the canteen and let a small amount trickle into his throat. He needed water, but the bourbon *was* good, so he swallowed some more before handing the canteen back to his captor.

"Good, thank you ... but I need water..."

"All in good time, my man!" Taggart turned. "Jeffries, which one a you guys got the first aid pouch? Can't you see our guest is bleedin'?" He turned back to Ainsley. "They're good men in a firefight, but they ain't got much manners," he said apologetically, spreading his arms wide and shrugging his shoulders.

Ainsley was confused. This was like something out of the *Twilight Zone.* Did these guys really think he didn't remember they had killed Simon? Did they think he didn't remember them shooting at him, screaming at him, and chasing him all over the Wind River Range? Were they crazy?

Jeffries grabbed one of the other guys, a former corpsman, and shoved him over toward Ainsley. Making sure he stayed out of reach of Taggart, the man knelt in front of Ainsley and used the four-inch kit scissors to cut open the back of Ainsley's nylon ripstop cargo trousers.

"Sit down," he ordered, and Ainsley, who was weak and dizzy anyway, complied. The man cleaned the nasty cut, none too gently, then applied generic antibiotic ointment to the laceration before putting a compress over it, holding it in place with an Ace bandage.

"That's gonna need stitches," he remarked to nobody in particular, "but I can't do 'em here. What I need's in my big kit bag up at the camp."

"Jeffries, see if one of you has anything we can give our guest to restore his strength a little before we take him back to the camp. We need to take good care of him now, you hear?"

Jeffries gave him a strange look, but Taggart was talking to Ainsley again already and didn't notice.

"Now, nobody's going to hurt you, Mr. Ainsley ... and, yes, I know who you are."

"You killed Simon!" Ainsley blurted out. The reality of that horror descended on him all at once.

"We didn't *need* him," Taggart said gently, as if he were talking to a mentally challenged ten-year-old. "You're the one with the money, Mr. Ainsley, and you're the one who's going to finance my empire!" Taggart turned and walked away, raising the bourbon-filled canteen to his lips and taking a deep swallow. He was going to be rich!

* * *

Ainsley kept his mouth tightly shut. The leader of this group didn't seem to be wrapped too tight, and the others, especially the bastard who had slammed him to the ground, appeared to be scared to death of the guy. *Ransom? Is that what this lunatic had in mind? Did he really think Ainsley was going to turn over one red cent to a guy who had already shown that he was willing to kill anyone he didn't need? Fat chance!* As soon as the asshole got his hands on enough cash, he'd be as good as dead, too, Ainsley was sure of that. The only thing that was keeping him alive now was letting these lunatics think they were going to get a cash payout for him ... and he was going to buy as much time as he could.

Byron was no hero, nor was he an outdoorsman, but he was smart as a whip. Burl knew where the camp was located, and if Byron couldn't make it to the outpost, Burl would know they had left. Simon's body would be found if it hadn't been already, and Byron would know what to do. Nolan Shepard had a whole folder of security scenario protocols, and Byron's eidetic memory contained all of them. All Nick had to do was buy some time.

* * *

Byron lay back on the sleeping bag he had dragged out to the campfire. It was not as thick as he'd have preferred, and the air mattress he'd bought at the discount store had leaked down again. His whole body ached and he was sure he had a fever. The antibiotic ointment on the soles of his feet had not been very effective, and the skin on the soles was swollen and inflamed. To make matters worse, Nick and Simon had not returned and it would be dark soon. That was not like them, not like them at all.

Byron was sick. His mind was spinning and he could not concentrate. A fleeting thought about one of Nolan Shepard's security protocols crossed his mind like a stone being skipped across a pond, but it was gone before he could make any sense of it. His head sank back on the sleeping bag and he closed his aching eyes. Black dots swam beneath his eyelids, making him even dizzier. He had to retch, but he didn't even have the strength left to sit up ... it was all he could do to get his head clear of the edge of the sleeping bag before he lost it and hurled like a drunken sailor.

* * *

It took longer to get to the far side of the lake than Brad had anticipated. Finding the trail had been an exercise in futility before he had lined up the landmarks he had fixed in his head earlier, and even then it had been hellishly difficult to locate the blood trail among the stones. Here and there Brad found the edge of a boot print in the soil between stones, and the wet bottoms of rocks revealed where someone had dragged their feet and turned one over.

Brad and Ving stopped and built a tiny cairn of stones, the tiniest on the top arranged to indicate the direction of travel. It was a technique they had used before and one Jared would recognize. The cairn would enable Jared to close with them even faster, and then they could use his superior tracking skills to catch up with Taggart faster.

Tracking required every ounce of concentration Brad was able to muster, so he and Ving did not speak until one of them spotted another blood spot or scuff mark. When they did find something, they built another signal cairn and moved on. It was only during these short "breathers", while they were building the cairns, that Brad allowed himself the luxury of thinking ahead.

Taggart *had* to be thinking of holding Ainsley for ransom. Nothing else made any sense. Otherwise Taggart would have killed the billionaire out of hand. Same thing with robbery. If they just wanted to rob the guy, Ainsley would have been shot out of hand and they would have taken what they wanted. Another thought crossed Brad's mind and left him cold. Was Ainsley up here in the wilderness alone? Surely not, he would have a companion or two, probably a security detail. Where the hell were they?

Brad shook his head. He had to focus on Ainsley. Everything else was sheer conjecture. Ainsley he knew about, had seen with his own eyes. *Focus.*

CHAPTER FOUR

Day One, 1812 hours

Well pleased with the performance of the Sharps, Jared strolled into camp with the long-barreled antique over his shoulder and a smile on his lips ... until he saw Ving's griddle lying on the ground beside the campfire. Instantly his every sense went into combat mode. He dropped the Sharps from his shoulder and loaded a cartridge in the chamber then flipped the safety strap off the holster bearing the eight-inch Colt Python he favored for recreational shooting.

His eyes picked up the note fastened to his tent flap, but he remained frozen in place, straining to hear the slightest thing out of the ordinary. Simultaneously, his nostrils flared, trying to pick up any odor that might be out of place. The only things he detected were the congealing grease on Ving's griddle, the slightly musty smell of the tents, and the faint odor of the burnt wood in the stone-lined fire pit.

Satisfied that there was no imminent threat, Jared stepped over and snatched Brad's note from his tent. He read it through then read it through again. He knew who Ainsley was and what he looked like; Fly had a pile of tech magazines on her working desk back at the ranch and he knew she was an admirer of the man. The name that jumped off the page of the note at him was Harlan Taggart.

He knew Taggart, and he despised him ... there was bad blood between them, had been ever since the second battle of Fallujah. Jared had an old score he'd like to settle with the scumbag, and this looked like the perfect opportunity. There was no question in his mind that whatever Taggart was up to, it did not bode well for Ainsley.

Jared stared up at the cloudless sky. There would be a full moon tonight, and without cloud cover, tracking should be easy enough. Brad had said in the note that he had contacted Fly about getting in contact with the proper authorities but that he and Ving needed to try to intervene before it was too late.

The description of the last known location of Taggart and Ainsley Brad had written in the note was detailed and precise, so Jared entered his tent to retrieve his copy of the 1:25,000 topographic map of the Wind River Range. He folded the laminated map sheet and stuffed it into the cargo pocket of his trousers and then grabbed several boxes of .357 ammo for the Python and stuffed them in his day pack. The ammo for his Sharps was heavy as hell, but that didn't stop him from stashing a couple of dozen rounds in the day pack as well as refilling the loops in the cartridge belt he had been using earlier. He was a firm believer in the premise that one could never have too much ammo.

For just a moment, he toyed with the idea of taking along the Thompson Center Contender he had brought along. The presentation box held the weapon and three different barrels, each of a different caliber, but he hadn't brought much ammunition for the weapon. He knew Brad and Ving were too smart to engage a superior force with inadequate firepower, and they only had their hunting rifles and handguns.

Whatever was going to happen, it wasn't going to be a pitched battle. Deciding the Thompson would be of little use, Jared reached instead for a handful of packs of beef jerky. Then he rolled up a Gore-Tex jacket and gloves, storing them in the bulging day pack, and crawled outside the tent. The last thing he took from his A.L.I.C.E. pack was a resealable plastic bag full of his special cocoa mix.

Checking his canteen and finding it full, Jared started to make for the far side of the lake, but then he stopped. Taking Brad's note, he added two lines to it for the guide Brad had arranged to meet them in two days' time, and then fastened it once more to the outside of the tent. Satisfied that he had covered as many bases as he could with the information and resources available to him, Jared set off at a fast pace.

He was looking forward to helping Nicholas Ainsley, it sounded like the man needed it. According to the note, Brad thought the man was injured as well. Jared smiled a thin, grim smile. Chasing an injured and apparently unarmed multibillionaire in the wilderness, with five-to-one odds no less; sounded like Taggart all right. Scum! It would be good to get a chance to settle up with the bastard ... and Jared hoped like hell he would fight back hard enough.

Taggart was a true incorrigible in every sense of the word. There was only one cure for what was wrong with him in Jared's estimation, and that was killing. He sped up his pace, eager to catch up with

Brad and Ving. They had a four-hour head start on him, and it was a good ten klicks over some rocky terrain before he would reach the spot Brad had indicated on the other side of the trout lake, where the trail began.

* * *

They were pushing him hard up the steep rocky grade, and he kept falling down, stumbling over the loose stones. He was weak from blood loss ... the field compress the corpsman had slapped on his calf had been leaking for a couple of hours. Nick was lucid enough to be pleased that he was slowing their march, but he knew he was pissing the men off. The leader had left an hour before, going on ahead and taking all of the men except the one he'd called Jeffries and the corpsman with him.

"For Christ's sake, pick your damned feet up," Jeffries barked at him as he stumbled and fell once again. "At this rate we ain't gonna get to base camp before tomorrow!"

It was already getting dark, and the temperature was dropping fast. Nick was beginning to think he was going to die out here in this wilderness, that he'd never see home again ... just like Simon. He was just about to say the hell with it, give up, and lie down on the scree when the corpsman caught up with him and made him sit.

"Let me look at that," he said, raising Nick's pants leg and fiddling with the Ace bandage.

"C'mon! We're only a couple hundred meters away from the base camp now, dammit! You can fix him up there, Jones. I'm tired an' I'm hungry an' I want a drink." Jeffries was whining and irritable.

"If you don't let me give this guy some attention right now we're gonna be draggin' a corpse into base camp, Jeffries ... and Taggart ain't gonna like it one little bit if you kill this guy off. He ain't worth a damn to us dead and you know it." Jones' fingers were deft and sure as he cleaned around the wound and replaced the compress. He tossed the bloody used compress and bandage carelessly onto the scree and wrapped a fresh Ace bandage over the new compress.

"There, that should get us the rest of the way in." He frowned as he turned to Jeffries. "If we don't get this thing sewed up real soon and get this guy some penicillin he ain't gonna make it. He's feverish, and that's bad in this cold. He needs somethin' warm to drink an' he needs rest."

"Then quit babyin' him an' let's get movin', Jones."

Jones ignored him and unscrewed the cap on his canteen, tilting it up to Nick's lips. It was the best he could do at the moment. "Just a little bit farther, fella, an' you can get some hot food an' some rest. Think you can make it?"

Nick nodded weakly and staggered to his feet ... a good trick considering they had his hands bound together behind his back. Did they really think he was capable of making an escape in his condition? They had to be crazy.

He lost track of time as he pushed on, every bone in his body crying out each time he lifted one of his feet and set it down. He heard the noise from the camp before he ever saw it. They passed a sloppily built wall made of fairly large stones, and then he saw a campfire sunk into a hollowed-out spot in the stone. In the darkness he could make out several tents around the fire, big Army tents. Each one was sitting on a leveled-out space on the slope, and each had a low wall around the outside. Nick could see that the camp was built on what appeared to be the remains of some sort of ancient village. He knew he was high up on a mountain, the air was thin and it was cold, but he had never heard of any ancient villages being located at this altitude.

"Our guest has arrived!" Taggart was standing in front of the fire, holding up a tin cup of what Nick was certain was not coffee. The man's words were slightly slurred. "Be nice to the man, boys, he's gonna finance our move to someplace a lot more comfortable!" There was raucous laughter from the men around the fire, but Nick was too exhausted to notice any more.

Strong hands pushed him none to gently into one of the tents and onto a sleeping bag. Jones brought him in a tin cup of warm stew, a hunk of bread, and a cup of strong, black coffee.

"I know it's going to be hard to do," Jones whispered, "but you need to eat this. After you take as much as you can, I'm going to stitch you up and you can get some sleep."

Groggy, Nick stared at the man.

"Why?"

Jones shook his head.

"Don't ask questions, man. The less you say around here the better off you're gonna be. Taggart don't play around. He needs you alive and well, but if he decides you ain't gonna net him a big payday, he'll kill you. You just need to be as cooperative as you can." He cocked his head to one side. "You hearin' me, man? That guy is a stone killer. You need to make him believe your company is going to pay big to get you back. If you don't convince him that's the case, you're going to be as dead as your friend."

* * *

Jared found the cairn on the flats above the lake while the sun was still above the horizon, but daylight was fading fast. He could see the faint blood trail, and he immediately followed it, chewing on one of his strips of beef jerky as he ran, the heavy, cumbersome Sharps slung across his back and slapping at his tailbone. He ignored it. A lot of ground had to be covered before twilight made it too hard to follow the trail. He would have to sit for a while until the moon rose enough for him to spot the larger spots and the cairns lest he lost the track.

Patience is a critical skill requirement for a combat tracker. Losing the track would mean a lot of wasted time circling around until he picked it up again. He hoped that Brad and Ving would slow or stop before they ended up lost. Ving was a damn good tracker, but he wasn't as good as Jared.

He ran quickly, spotting the cairns, trail signs he, Brad, and Ving had worked out over the years, each one leaving information that only one of the three of them would understand. When twilight fell, Jared settled down to wait for the moon to rise high enough for him to see clearly enough to continue. Patches of frost were going to make it a tad more difficult to follow the trail, but Jared had the pattern of the cairns down now, and he knew that they would be closer together and easier to spot.

He scratched out a spot on the rocky ground, a depression big enough for a heat tab and his canteen cup, and lit the heat tab. The U.S. military had discontinued the use of heat tabs, transitioning instead to the Flameless Ration Heater (FRH), a water-activated exothermic reaction item that produces heat, but many people, including the members of Team Dallas, didn't think they got hot enough. There was a huge surplus of heat tabs after the transition, and they were available on the civilian market.

The faint blue glow of the compressed trioxane tablet would not give away his position, if anyone was watching, and he needed the sugar in his makin's to replenish his energy. Chewing on another strip of jerky as he waited for the water to come to a boil, his eyes constantly scanning for movement around him, his thoughts turned to his last encounter with Taggart, in Fallujah in December of 2004.

The Seabees had disrupted the power in the city and two Marine Regimental Combat Teams (RCTs) augmented by three seven-man SEAL Sniper Teams were deployed. Jared's platoon from 1st Recon was tasked to provide advance reconnaissance in the city. Needless to say, with all the different forces involved in the attack, the tactical situation was total chaos.

Jared had found a two-story building that was only partially demolished by an earlier artillery bombardment and climbed the ruins to make a sniper's nest so that he could provide cover for the other men, who were conducting a house-to-house search for insurgents.

The Barrett .50 was a real beast, and the climb into the nest was hard as hell. By the time Jared was set up, his spotter was already tapping his shoulder frantically and pointing out a crew-served weapon that was raking the streets with heavy fire. The

Marines of 1ˢᵗ Recon were returning fire as best they could, but the insurgents had them pinned down with enfilade fire.

Jared nestled his cheek against the stock of the Barrett and fixed his scope reticle on the gunner, whose head was barely visible above the sandbags around his position some three hundred meters up the long, narrow street. He took a deep breath, let half of it out, and the reticle stopped its wobbly dance and rested on the top of the gunner's head. He squeezed the match trigger gently and the round, as it was supposed to, surprised him when it detonated in the chamber. The field of vision in the scope was filled with a spray of red and the automatic weapon ceased to fire.

The Recon Marines immediately rushed forward and Jared and his spotter sought other targets. It happened fast, and Jared and his spotter found themselves alone in the street that a moment ago had been filled with flying lead.

"Shit! Saddle up, Jake, we gotta get after those boys before they end up in another fix!" The two of them shimmied down to the ground floor, lugging the heavy Barret with them. By the time they made it back into the narrow street, an element of one of the RCTs that had apparently lost its way were rounding up a handful of terrified non-combatants that Recon had left behind.

"Get down, raghead!" A stocky, muscular gunnery sergeant kicked one of the civilians in the ass, knocking him to the ground. The other Marines in the gunny's squad were looking away in embarrassment, but they were apparently as afraid of the gunny as the civilians were. One of the civilians, a female, shrieked as she watched the man fall and began to run towards the gunny.

Jared, running toward the melee, watched in horror as the gunny swiveled and fired from the hip, catching the shrieking woman in the chest. He tackled the gunny from behind, taking him to the ground. As he struggled to get the weapon away from the lunatic, he was wrestled down by a couple of men from the gunny's squad.

"Let it be, Sarge. Taggart's crazy as hell, but he's one of us."

"I don't give a flyin' shit, Marine! He just murdered a damn civilian in cold blood! We're s'posed ta be the fuckin' *good guys*!"

Taggart got to his feet, sneering, and recovered his weapon.

"Good guys hell, this is a *war*, Marine, and them are just a bunch a no good camel-humpers that don't mean shit!"

"They're *civilians*, Gunny," Jared said hoarsely.

"Ah hell," Taggart said and lashed out with the toe of his boot, catching Jared square on the jaw and knocking him out cold. "Come on gyrenes, leave that pussy where he lays ... we got us a war to fight." He turned his back on Jared and marched off. The other Marines in his squad followed reluctantly, and none of them looked back.

Jared came to in the dust several minutes later, his jaw swollen and aching. He saw his spotter lying on the ground several feet away, unconscious, and crawled over to check on him. It was only then that he noticed the Barrett was gone. He never found out whether Taggart and his men had taken it or whether one of the civilians had made off with it while he was unconscious. The body of the woman was gone, and only her bloodstains remained to mark the place of her murder.

CHAPTER FIVE

Day One, 2117 hours

"I shoulda brung my gloves," Ving grumbled. It was getting cold and the rough stones were scraping his big fingers raw as he stacked them on the cairn.

"That's gonna have to be the last one for tonight, Ving. I can't see the track anymore; my eyes aren't what they were when I was a kid."

"Shit, you an' me both! When we was back in the Sandbox, we woulda already caught up with that sonofabitch by now."

Both men were in remarkable physical condition, but they knew their limitations, and they well knew that rest was a weapon. Both were smart enough to know that if they lost the trail, the time lost might cost Ainsley his life … or they could lose their own if they stumbled upon Taggart and his men in the dark.

"They had more than an hour's head start on us, Ving. We can scoop out a hole and at least make a cup of joe."

"Roger that! My hands is achin' from stackin' all them stones. Sure hope Jared 'preciates all my efforts."

"I'll appreciate it if he just gets here. Hope he can follow the cairns all right."

Ving squinted at the man he knew better than any other man on Earth.

"You kiddin', right? Jared could follow fish farts in a river an' never lose a step. That boy's half coonhound and half ghost."

Both men laughed quietly, both busily scooping out a hollow large enough to permit their canteen cups to rest below the surface of the ground. It was hard going, the ground rocky and unforgiving. They stacked small stones in the hole to raise the cups high enough to get the compressed trioxane tablets underneath them. Brad lay down in front of the hole as Ving cupped his hand around a waterproof match and struck it. He let the flame flare just long enough to catch the heat tab and then snuffed it out. The faint blue glow of the flame gave off very little light, but they were taking no chances.

"Ainsley's bleedin' worse now. He's prob'ly slowin' 'em down considerable," Ving said quietly.

"I'm surprised they're not taking better care of him, Ving. I've been thinking, and the only reason I can come up with for them chasing him is that they recognized him and they think they can ransom him for a butt-load of cash…"

"You're prob'ly right, but don't forget who's ramroddin' that bunch. That Taggart's a lowlife scumbag and he don't give a crap about nothin' or nobody but himself; that man's a sho' nuff devil an' that's the stone truth."

Brad fell silent, his mind traveling back, back to Fallujah and Operation Phantom Fury.

* * *

"Captain Lingenfelter wants to see you, Gunny."

"What for?"

"Hell if I know, he just said tell you he wants to see you in the CP ASAP."

Brad sighed and got wearily to his feet. Bob Lingenfelter was a good C.O., and he had a great respect for the guy. There was no question in his mind that the captain would make major soon, and the company would lose him ... he was that good. He knew the C.O. wouldn't have sent for him if it wasn't necessary, they had both been busy clearing the north side of the city of Fallujah since dawn, and casualties had been high. The Second Battle of Fallujah was turning out to be a bloodbath of gigantic proportions, by far the worst fighting

Brad and his Recon Marines had seen yet. He groaned and made his way to the C.P.

"Come on in, Brad, don't stand there and knock at the tent flap like some boot."

"Yes sir!" Brad entered and Captain Lingenfelter motioned to a stainless pitcher of coffee sitting on the collapsible wooden field desk.

"Grab a mug and help yourself. This won't take long." Lingenfelter looked exhausted, dark bags under his tired eyes.

Brad did as he was told, grateful for the strong black coffee. It was hot, and it tasted amazing.

"A sensitive situation has been ... tasked to me, Brad," Lingenfelter said in his deep voice. "One that offends my sense of honor and will reflect badly on the Corps if we don't find a solution posthaste."

Brad glanced up from his mug, surprised. Lingenfelter was a by-the-book kind of guy when it came to matters of honor and the dignity of the Corps ... and he wasn't one for playing politics.

"Battalion says they have reports of a gunny that's gone off the rails. They have no proof, but the rumors are that he and his squad have gotten separated from their parent unit and are committing random ... atrocities in our sector. I'm going to level with you, Brad, if I had one shred of proof, I would tell the colonel to go to hell and send the MPs after this guy, turn him over myself and have him court-martialed ... but we don't even have a name. I would go to NCIS with this, but the old man expressly forbid me to do that. I don't like it one bit, but we have to find this guy and run him out of our A.O. (Area of Operations.)"

"What do you need me to do, sir?"

"Hit the streets with a squad and an interpreter, take Zamir, first thing in the morning. Track him down. If you catch him in the act, whatever it might be, take him forcibly into custody and I'll turn him in to the M.P.s myself. If you don't, I'm sure you and your friend Sergeant Ving can find a way to 'persuade' him to get the hell out of my A.O. and get back to his unit. Then they can deal with him."

"Will do, sir!"

"And Brad ... if I have to say this, thank you. I don't know another NCO whose judgement I would trust on this. Keep it under your hat."

"Yes sir!"

* * *

The streets were still chaotic, the fighting intense and deadly, but Brad forged ahead anyway. Small insurgent groups gave them fierce but brief opposition.

"Second door down on the left! Hostiles!" Brad barked. He fired at the doorway, causing the gunman to duck back inside.

"Spurgeon, take Alpha Team and cover the back! Randolph, on me!" Brad hugged the stone and mud wall, his CAR-4 at the ready, and made his way toward the doorway.

"Behind you, Brad!" Ving shouted, a three-round burst spitting from his own weapon. A dark-robed shooter fell from a rooftop across the street. "Bastards are ever'where!"

Spurgeon's voice came over Brad's com.

"Got it locked down, they ain't getting out this way!"

Brad's back pressed against the wall next to the doorway, his heart racing. Reaching down to the cargo pocket of his utilities, he brought out an Enhanced Diversionary Device (flash-bang grenade), pulled the pin, and back-handed it through the doorway. He didn't have to tell his men to *go* when the device detonated, they were experienced, and the terrifying drill was routine these days. He was the third man through the door, but the two Marines ahead of him had already eliminated the insurgent, who lay sprawled on the floor, riddled with 5.56 rounds.

"Clear!"

Once again, no commands were necessary. The insurgent's clothing and body were searched as the rest of the squad converged on the apartment and carefully searched it for booby traps, weapons, and any documents, maps, or photographs of intelligence value. As was too often the case, they found nothing other than the U.S. M-16 and several fully charged magazines the insurgent had been carrying.

"Zamir! Question the neighbors, find out what they can tell us about this guy and see if you can find some willing to testify against him when we catch him ... and don't forget to ask about our rogue gunny." Brad stared down at the dead insurgent, marveling yet again that the only way to tell an insurgent from a civilian was whether he was armed or not.

Worse yet, many civilians carried weapons just to protect themselves. It was a hell of a note. There was no foolproof way to differentiate between combatants and non-combatants other than deciding who was shooting at you. All wars are confusing, but the insurgents were comprised of several hundred militias, some uniformed, most not ... and they were fighting each other as well as the American-led coalition. It was no damned wonder the civilians policed up weapons after firefights and carried them to protect themselves and their families.

Zamir came through the front door, an unpleasant look on his swarthy face.

"Sayyid, the neighbors, they will not speak in front of you. I was told they will not trust anyone who wears this emblem..." Zamir reached out and tapped the eagle, globe, and anchor stenciled on the breast pocket of Brad's blouse. He was furious … and embarrassed because he took great pride in working for the Corps, and he truly admired Brad's integrity, abilities, and the way he looked after his troops.

"I was afraid of that."

Zamir smiled tentatively.

"Please do not take offense, Sayyid, they do not trust anyone in any uniform, even members of Iraqi Security Forces (ISF). They do not even trust each other." Zamir looked down at the rubble-covered dirt floor in shame. "It was not always thus."

"This is going to be harder than I thought," Brad muttered under his breath. "Tell me what they told you, Zamir."

"Not much, Sayyid. They did say his uniform bore the same emblem as yours, and the description included the cloth badge of rank … also the same as yours. They say he is شيطان, *Shaitan* himself, but his men call him Taggit or Taggot, something like that."

Brad stared back at Zamir impassively.

"Did they tell you what he did specifically?"

"They say he is a despoiler of children, Sayyid. He and his men kill without warning and for no reason. *Shaitan* himself steals anything of value, and anything he leaves behind, especially food, is scattered in the dust, no longer fit for consumption." Zamir's face was contorted in anger. "These people are starving, Sayyid, near death, and they have nothing left and no place to go that is safe."

Brad thought for a moment then turned to Spurgeon.

"Collect all the MREs (Meal, Ready to Eat) we have and give them to Zamir. We can afford to miss a few meals."

It was done quickly and quietly, without any hesitation or resentment. It was not the first time they had given all they had, and, to a man, they were proud to serve under this particular gunny. Spurgeon put the plastic packets into a waterproof bag, and then the men added the remnants of the accessory packs they carried loose in their pockets—chewing gum, instant coffee, salt, sugar, hot sauce, toilet paper.

"Crap!" Brad muttered. "I forgot! Zamir, make sure we didn't give them any pork products."

Zamir grinned.

"It is well, Sayyid. Not all the people here are Muslim, though they are in the majority." He said it kindly, not adding that Brad should have known that by now. The gunny, compassionate and intelligent as he was, was still a foreigner. How could he possibly remember everything?

"Tell them I will send a few cases of MREs back here as soon as we get back to headquarters. Tell them I am sorry we do not have more with us."

* * *

They fought every inch of the way, constantly battling snipers and small groups of militants, avoiding the larger ones. Everywhere they went, they faced the same fear and mistrust, and Zamir got the same results: tales of depravity and atrocities, and a hundred variations of the real name of the man they called *Shaitan*.

* * *

"We got to get the hell outta this A.O., Taggart." The lanky Tennessean, a lance corporal, squared off with his gunny, something he was loathe to do because, as far as he was concerned, the man was crazy. When they had first gotten separated from their unit in the chaos and fury of Operation Phantom Fury, slipping out of the rigid strictures of the Corps, something the young man had never really adjusted to, had seemed like a lark.

Taggart had seemed larger than life, kinda like Marlon Brando in *Apocalypse Now*, a movie he had watched a dozen times or more. It had been kicky, a blast. They had been able to do anything they wanted with total impunity. No more shaving every morning, no standing formation, no shit details, no guard mount, and, best of all, no officers lording it over them and making life miserable. But lately, Taggart seemed to have gone off the deep end, doing shit none of them approved of … and he was getting worse every day.

Taggart's face grew red and his eyes bulged.

"What the hell are you talking about, McLean?" he roared.

"Gunny, there's a guy looking for you ... for us. Another gunny, an' he's Force Recon! Word is he's lookin' to take you in, all of us really, an' you know what that means. Freakin' Leavenworth!" *If he doesn't just shoot us out of hand!* McLean didn't vocalize that particular thought. Force Recon was a collection of seriously bad dudes, and rumor had it they worked closely with NCIS and CIA. NCIS wasn't so bad, but CIA, those dudes were into some serious bad-assery. They *killed* people for less than what they had done with Taggart.

Taggart's eyes glazed over.

"Who else have you talked to about this, McLean?"

"Nobody, Gunny, honest! I heard it from Mahmud an' I come straight to you with it. Swear to God!"

Mahmud was a local black marketer who dealt in expressly forbidden alcoholic beverages, weed, and cocaine; the booze was cheap rotgut and expensive as hell. The weed and coke were cheaper than beer in the States.

"You sure? Nobody else?"

"Honest Gunny, not another living soul!"

Mclean never saw the Kabar coming. He felt the shock in his chest and barely had time to see the hilt, angled downward, protruding from beneath his sternum before he collapsed, DRT (Dead Right There).

Taggart glanced around to make sure no one had seen him then bent down and grabbed Mclean's body by the shoulders and dragged him into a tiny alleyway off the street. Grasping the Kabar in both hands, he drew it out of McLean's body and wiped the blade off on the man's blouse. Then he crept back to the corner and peered out to make absolutely certain none of the squad had seen him. Satisfied that his treacherous act had not been witnessed, he then stepped into the street and began to bellow out an alarm at the top of his lungs. The squad poured out of the single-room dwelling where they had been lounging, clothing in disarray but weapons in hand.

"He got McLean! He went that way!" Taggart pointed down the alleyway, and the squad rushed past the still form of McLean without a second glance.

"Bastards!" Taggart growled. They hadn't even stopped to check on McLean. Marines left no man behind, that was a given. The irony of the situation eluded him. He walked over and knelt down by McLean's body.

"Sorry buddy, he whispered. "You would have fucked up everything and I couldn't allow that." He covered the young man's face, as much to keep everyone from seeing the look of shock on the corpse's face as to provide him with dignity in death. His brain racing, he began to formulate a plan that would get him out of the fix he was in with his butt intact ... and he would do it, by God, even if it meant killing off the whole squad. The longer he thought about it the more it seemed that would be the best solution anyway—and that's exactly what he did.

* * *

"Foxtrot Romeo Seven, this is Foxtrot Romeo Fiver Bravo, over..."

"Bravo, this is Foxtrot Romeo Seven, over."

"Foxtrot Romeo Seven, Fiver wants you to report to Charlie Papa ASAP, over."

"This is Foxtrot Romeo Seven, Roger, Wilco, out."

"Saddle up. We've gotta get back to the CP ASAP."

"What's up, Gunny?" Spurgeon was a good team leader. He knew it would be up to him to assume command of the patrol if something were to happen to Brad, and it was his responsibility to ask if the information was not volunteered. A patrol leader had a hell of a lot of responsibilities, and he had to depend on his subordinate leaders to help keep track of the details.

"You know as much as I do, Spurgeon. The old man wants us back, we go back."

"Roger that, Gunny!"

The men automatically assumed their positions in their urban travel formation, moving down the blighted city streets, past the destruction caused by artillery and aircraft bombardment. They caught sight of furtive movements in the dark alleys and on some of the rooftops, but they arrived back at the CP unmolested.

"Break 'em down, clean the weapons, and then check with me before you fall 'em out for chow and showers, Spurgeon."

"Roger that, Gunny!"

Brad turned and headed toward the company CP, tired and dirty after days of fruitless drudgery looking for *Shaitan* in the north end of the bloody hell that was Fallujah.

"Reporting sir!" He didn't bother to even pretend to knock at the tent flap. Captain Lingenfelter was sitting at his field desk, the ubiquitous stainless pitcher of hot coffee sitting beside two heavy china mugs.

"Take a load off, Gunny," Lingenfelter said, not unsympathetically. He still looked exhausted himself. Brad knew that the colonel kept his company commanders busy as hell.

"What's up, sir?"

"Your mission is over, Brad. The scumbag you were looking for showed up at the Brigade TOC (Tactical Operations Center) this afternoon with a wild ass tale about getting wounded and trapped 'behind the lines.' He reported his whole squad as K.I.A."

"Who the hell was he?"

"Gunnery Sergeant Harlan Taggart, RCT-7, 3rd Marines."

"Taggart, not Taggit or Taggot," Brad muttered under his breath. "Wounded?"

"Ahhh!" Lingenfelter made a dismissive gesture of disgust with one hand. "A scratch. Said he got it in hand-to-hand with a militant. I've cut myself worse dry shaving."

"That's his whole story?"

"That's all the S2 (Battalion Intelligence) could get out of him. G-2 is taking a shot at him now, but he's a crafty bastard. Whatever the hell he's been up to, I'm afraid he's going to get away with it."

Brad sighed.

"I'm a firm believer in karma, sir. Sooner or later, it's all going to catch up with him."

"God, I hope so."

"I just hope I get a chance to give karma a helping hand."

"Amen to that, Gunny. Amen to that."

CHAPTER SIX

Day Two, 0214 hours

It had been a long ass day, and he would never admit it, but he was flagging. That's probably why he almost missed them. The sugar rush from his cocoa makin's had turned into a sugar crash because he'd been so eager to catch up with Brad and Ving that he'd failed to take the time to stop and refuel along the way ... and he knew better. A good tracker had to be able to establish a balance between the need for speed, the need to maintain a constant state of alertness, and to extend his endurance. As a consequence of his excessive eagerness, he had been unable to maintain the balance and he had taken far too long to catch up with them ... and still he had almost missed them.

Jared had misstepped, and his booted foot had grazed a softball-sized stone, making a clicking sound that made Brad sit up and rotate into a prone firing position, his accurized .45 aimed at the shadowy figure he quickly recognized as Jared.

"Getting' sloppy in your old age, Jared!"

Already annoyed, Jared's discomfort grew when he heard Ving snicker quietly in the background. He hadn't even noticed the behemoth until then.

"I ain't getting' old, I just made a tenderfoot mistake an' let myself get a mite tuckered out," he snorted quietly. "Coupla hours shuteye an' some a my makin's an' I'll be good ta go."

"Couple more years an' you gonna need to jack up that haircut a yours and drive a new body under it," Ving chuckled. "You ain't thirty no more, Jared."

"At least I'll still *have* hair in a coupla more years," Jared retorted. Lately he had taken to teasing Ving about his receding hairline ... teasing him so badly that Ving had started cutting it so short that his blue-black scalp could be clearly seen through the crinkly curls of hair on his head.

Jared found a bare spot on the ground and squatted down on his haunches to scrape out a hollow for his heat tab. When he had the hollow shaped just to his liking, he scrabbled around for two stones that suited his purpose and arranged them on either side of the hollow so that his canteen cup would rest directly above the unlit segment of heat tab he had laid down on the bare spot at the bottom of the hollow. Brad and Ving watched, as they always did, in total fascination, as Jared went through his unvarying ritual preparation of his makin's.

Jared popped the snaps on his canteen cover one at a time and then lifted the Korean War era aluminum canteen out and set it on the ground beside his makeshift stove. Then he dug into the canteen cover again and lifted out a stainless steel G.I. canteen cup, which he carefully set on the ground by the canteen. From his breast pocket, Jared removed a G.I. spoon that had once been part of a mess kit and laid it across the top of the canteen cup. Then he produced a moist towelette out of an MRE accessory packet from another pocket and peeled it open (Brad had once seen him use a fresh triangle bandage G.I.s refer to as a 'drive-on rag'). Jared proceeded to wash both spoon and cup thoroughly, set the spoon inside the cup, and set the cup atop the makeshift field stove.

Unscrewing the cap from the canteen cup, he lifted the spoon in one hand as he poured water into the cup until his calibrated eye told him it had reached the precise level he required. Then he struck a waterproof paper match to the heat tab and removed his Ziploc bag of makin's and slid the little zipper back, opening the bag.

"Got ta sprinkle this stuff in a little at a time ta make sure I end up with a solution instead of a suspension," he said in a low voice, his focus on the canteen cup. "Scientist fella tol' me that a long time ago ... same fella that tol' me a little cayenne pepper would bring out the flavor of the chocolate. Smart guy..."

"Sometimes I think our boy is about one sammich short of a picnic, Brad," Ving muttered, amused.

"We all have our quirks, Ving. I know this guy, been knowing him a long time now, he's the same way about bacon, of all things. How's that for freaky?"

"Low blow, Brad, low blow. That was below the belt..."

The good-natured banter helped to ease the tension they all felt, but all three men were acutely aware of the plight of Nicholas Ainsley.

"You think Taggart is gonna kill Ainsley, don't ya?"

"I think he's going to eventually. That's his solution, as I recall, to problems that are likely to send him to prison. Remember Fallujah?"

Ving snorted. "Course I do. Captain Lingenfelter never believed a word Taggart said about his squad being K.I.A. an' neither did we!"

"Nope, and he got away with it that time. They caught up with him a while back and sent him to Leavenworth. Appears he was up to his old tricks ... on his third tour I read."

"I heard 'bout that. Wonder what he's doin' way hell out here? I thought he was locked up."

"I asked Fly to find out about that when I called before we left camp. She said she'll have the information for me when I call back in the morning."

"I hope you told her to send some ordnance. I don't like surprises, an' like the ol' man said back in the day, Taggart's a crafty bastard. No tellin' what he's got up his sleeve."

"I gave her a short list, and I told her not to tell Vicky and the others any more than she absolutely had to. I don't really think we're gonna need them, the ordnance is just a precaution."

"Good luck with her not tellin' Vicky anything. But sendin' them gadgets a hers is a great idea. They sure would come in handy…"

Brad raised his hand in an indifferent gesture. "I asked her to send the earwigs and a couple of the smaller drones along with the ordnance, Ving, and I told her to set up an air drop. We'll have to set out early enough to find Taggart's camp and then back off to send her the coordinates. Don't want that snake to have any idea we're anywhere around."

"If we don't lose the trail…"

"I won't lose the trail, Ving. I want that sonofabitch…" Jared was bent over his canteen cup, his nostrils flaring as he savored the aroma of his special blend of cocoa. His features screwed into a mask of anger and disgust at the memory of the murder of the innocent Iraqi woman in Fallujah and his own subsequent brutalization in the street. The stories he'd heard afterward about Taggart's depredations had horrified him and left him guilt-ridden. He had been too slow that day, he should have taken Taggart down. Who knew how many innocents had died because he, Jared Smoot, had been too slow? He had lived with the shame of it for years. Oh yes, Harlan Taggart was going down.

Brad Jacobs had been an outstanding Marine, and he was perhaps the finest man Jared had ever known, but he had too much faith in the system … and the system had failed with Harlan Taggart. Sure, they'd tried and convicted him, yet here he was in the wilds of Wyoming, still up to no good. Jared could still see Taggart's face clearly in his mind's eye, only this time it was sitting atop the sight post on the Sharps.

Brad leaned back on his butt pack, which he was using as a pillow on the hard, rocky ground. He pulled his poncho over his legs, having left the tents in camp. They hadn't wanted anything to slow them down, so they were traveling light.

"I just hope we locate Taggart's camp in the morning. This is big country, and there's no telling how far off the grid Taggart and his crew are staying."

"If Ainsley's hurt as bad as you seem to think he was, I doubt they would have taken him far."

"We don't even know for sure if they didn't just kill him out of hand."

"Dead men don't leave blood trails, Brad," Jared said reasonably.

"I must be more tired than I thought. That never occurred to me."

"Looks like Jared ain't the only one gittin' old, Brad!" Ving chuckled and rolled over on his side. He was feeling his age too, and he was determined to catch a little shut-eye before morning. He dreamed, of course, of bacon. Piles and piles of crisp, tasty bacon.

Brad had one final thought before drifting off to sleep. *There's no telling how long this is going to take. I need to turn the sat phone off to conserve power. Fly is going to hate me for this, but I can't afford to take a chance on this phone dying when I need it most.* He lifted the sat phone up, stared at it for a moment, and then turned it off.

* * *

A dangerously high fever had taken him, brought on by the infection in his feet. Byron moaned, tossing and turning in his sleeping bag. He was so fitful that he hadn't bothered to unzip the bag, and he was sweating profusely inside of it. His clothes and the bag itself were soaked, and the cold was seeping in.

The fever brought with it delirium. Byron slipped in and out of consciousness, though he was not lucid by any means when he woke. He was a city dweller, not an outdoorsman. His experience at camping consisted of two weeks at summer camp when he was twelve (which he'd hated), and a single sleepover in his best friend's back yard when he was fourteen. In short, he was singularly unsuited for his present circumstances. He had agreed to come along with Nick and Simon because he'd wanted to impress his bosses ... and that desire might well end up killing him. Not that he was aware of the fact. He was busy fighting off hungry wolves in his delirium. He had no way of knowing of Simon's death or Nick's abduction. He was not even aware that they weren't back in camp yet.

Day Two, 0603 hours

"What does he want with me?" Nick was groggy, but he wanted to engage the guy who brought in breakfast for him in conversation if he could. The man was in his thirties and obviously had a military background. Whipcord thin and tough-looking, he was freshly shaved and his hair was cut in a style known as 'high and tight' by the Marines from Camp Pendleton. Nick had seen enough of them to be familiar with it.

"You'll have to ask him, mister." The man was not talkative, setting a metal plate with fried eggs, trout, and a slightly overdone biscuit on it on the floor in front of Nick.

"I don't think I can eat that with my hands tied behind me." Nick leaned forward and twisted around to display his hands, white from lack of circulation and totally numb.

"Jesus!" the man exclaimed. "That dumb sonofabitch!" He swept out of the tent and was back moments later carrying a set of stainless steel handcuffs. "Stupid bastard! Jeffries was supposed to have Stevens put these on you last night." He removed a Kabar from its sheath on his belt and slipped it under the knot in Nick's bonds, lifting up until the rope parted. It didn't take much effort, the blade was razor sharp.

"There! Rub your hands until you get some circulation back." He stood there, three feet away, Kabar in hand, watching as Nick complied with his command. There was no mistaking it was a command, just as it was clear that the man was used to giving orders.

Rubbing his numb hands together did not bring immediate relief, it brought pain. Nick winced as he obeyed, but he didn't make a sound. When he finally managed to get some color back, the man sheathed his Kabar and snapped the handcuffs around his wrists with an ease that bespoke considerable experience with the device.

"M.P.?" Nick asked.

"You talk too much," the man said. Porter Hackman had been an M.P. at Pendleton, and he'd done two combat tours, one in Iraq and one in Afghanistan. He'd made the mistake of getting caught playing hide the salami with a girl who *said* she was eighteen (she wasn't) and who turned out to be the dependent child of a major assigned to the G-1 staff at Pendleton. That little escapade had resulted in a ten-year sentence in Leavenworth ... which didn't happen because he was lucky enough to be on the same prisoner detachment as Taggart.

He had gone along with the escape because it had appealed to him more than ten years in Leavenworth, but he didn't like Taggart and had intended to cut loose as soon as things settled down a bit. This business with Ainsley had prompted him to stick around a while longer, at least until he saw whether Taggart's big talk about ransoming this rich character paid off.

"Eat your chow. I'll be back with a cup of coffee in a second."

"Fork?" Nick asked.

"Eat with your hands, dumbass." Hackman was gone.

Nick's eyes scanned the inside of the tent. There was nothing he could use, the stone floor was bare. With a shrug of his aching shoulders, he picked up the piece of pan fried trout with his hands and began to eat. Despite the circumstances in which he found himself, Nick didn't think he'd ever tasted anything so good.

Hackman was back in no time, carrying a porcelain-covered steel cup that matched the plate, obviously part of a set, full of strong black coffee. He set it down and backed away again, a measured distance that left him in easy striking distance if Nick tried anything foolish. Nick was not a foolish man.

There's nothing I can do except bide my time. I'm hurt, I'm exhausted, and I wouldn't stand a chance with these guys ... they look tough as nails and they aren't in the least friendly. I need to eat, and I need to rest if they let me. I can only hope that Nolan follows the hostage protocol. He's been a good chief of security so far, but he hasn't really been tested yet.

Nick sighed, set the fish bones down on the plate, and lifted one of the fried eggs to his mouth. No salt, but he wasn't about to ask for any. He ate it anyway; he needed to build his strength up.

CHAPTER SEVEN

Day Two, 0600 hours

Fly Highsmith was worried. She had followed Brad's instructions and told Vicky very little other than that Brad had witnessed the (maybe) kidnapping of Nicholas Ainsley and had recognized Harlan Taggart, but the information she'd managed to acquire about Taggart from sources in the Intelligence community disturbed her. Harlan Taggart was an odious human being, and she was using the term human being loosely. By all accounts, he was a serious sociopath but a canny one.

He had been able to fool a lot of very bright people for a very long time before he finally slipped up, and then he had killed both guards on the prisoner pickup detail, leaving their bodies crammed into a trash chute in the men's room at Denver International Airport. The FBI and NCIS were following a multitude of leads at the moment, and as far as they were concerned, the one Fly had given them was unsubstantiated and therefore far down on their list of priorities.

Brad had been adamant about not mentioning the ordnance and equipment he wanted air-dropped, insisting that he just wanted it as a precaution. Fly did *not* like being put in the position of having to deceive Vicky and she intended to raise hell with Brad about it when he got back.

"Good morning, Fly! Thought you might want a cup of tea so I brought some out for you."

"Thanks, but I just made a cup of hot cocoa."

Vicky Chance, a tall, lithe woman with incredibly long legs, high, firm breasts, luminous jade-green eyes and incredibly long lashes, was Brad Jacobs' paramour and mistress of the manor house. She was an inveterate flirt, and her long, red hair and overall appearance drove men wild. She was also, as Fly had learned, as tough a female as she was a beautiful one. Vicky had been a C.I.D. special agent assigned to the 2nd Law Enforcement Battalion at Lejeune. When she separated from the Corps, she became a special agent with Immigration and Customs Enforcement (I.C.E.) assigned to the Human Trafficking team.

She had met Team Dallas at a resort in Mexico and had partnered with them in their mission to the Amazon, where she had been wounded. Despite her wound, she had completed the mission. By then she and Brad had formed what appeared to be a serious attachment and she had been invited to join the team.

"Oooooh, Jared left you some of his makin's!"

"Don't make anything out of it, Vicky, I just mentioned that I liked the aroma of the stuff and he left me a taste. That's all."

"Methinks thou doth protest too much," Vicky quipped, laughing.

"I'm a little worried, Vicky. Brad was supposed to check in this morning and he hasn't called me yet."

"I wouldn't worry about it, Fly. Those boys haven't taken a vacation in forever, and they're probably yukking it up and having a grand old time fishing and swapping tall tales."

"I don't know, he sounded pretty serious when he was talking about that Taggart character…"

"Have you called Ainsley's corporate offices yet?"

"Yes, and all I got was a prepared blurb about him being out of the office for two weeks and could they take a message. I swear it would be easier to get hold of the president of the United States!"

"Well, there you go! If he was in trouble they would know, wouldn't they? I've read about that guy, he's a big deal multi-billionaire and he has a big time security detail."

"I don't know…"

"I'm sure if there's real trouble Brad will call, Fly. He's a big boy, and with Ving and Jared along with him, I'd be more worried about that Taggart character if I was you."

Vicky smiled her dazzling supermodel smile and left the half-finished office, waving gaily over her shoulder.

I hope you're right. I don't like what I'm hearing about this Taggart character at all. He's a snake in the grass, and he's smart as hell, even if he is crazy. Jim Clancy in the FBI Field Office in Denver told me in confidence that Taggart and the guys that escaped with him at the airport are suspects in an armored car heist, but they haven't been able to confirm that yet. Got away with a bunch of cash and then disappeared.

If that was Taggart and his gang, they had a chunk of money to spend on what Brad calls 'ordnance', and money draws thugs like flies. It's all supposition at this point, but if you put it all together, kidnapping a fat target of opportunity like Nicholas Ainsley makes sense.

She shut down her laptop and finished her cocoa, which reminded her of Jared. The rangy Texan was sexy as hell, and it had been a very long time since she had taken a man to her bed. Fly shook her head roughly, shaking off her thoughts of Jared. She had an ordnance 'care package' to prepare from the stocks in the armory and she had the drones and earwigs to pack ... all of which had to fit in an air-droppable container.

The package also had to be put together without arousing Vicky's curiosity or Willona's. Willona Ving was sharp as a tack, and she had a clear view of the armory from her kitchen window. With a little luck, she would be too busy with Ving's two kids to notice Fly leaving the armory in one of the Mrazors with a heavy equipment bag in the cargo compartment.

As if that wasn't hard enough, she would have to get the container to the airport for shipment to Wyoming, another detail she had to arrange. It would have to go by private jet at an exorbitant price, and then she would have to arrange for a bush pilot to take the package from the Pinedale airport and drop it to Brad ... who, as it happened, would not be able to give her the drop coordinates until he called. Fly heaved an exasperated sigh. This was not going to be easy, but then that's why Brad paid her the big bucks. If it was an easy job, he could have hired anybody to do it.

* * *

Vicky was humming to herself when she got back into the house, thinking about Brad's cousin Jessica and Charlie. Jessica Paul, a gorgeous blonde with a killer body, had been an adventuress and treasure hunter before joining the team, proving herself on the missions to Alaska and Peru. Charlie Dawkins, a rawboned six footer with coal-black hair, deep blue eyes, and big hands, had spent years in the clandestine service of the Department of State. He had joined Brad's little band of merry men after collaborating with them on a mission to Alaska. He had proven himself under fire, and, incidentally, fallen head over heels for Jessica.

The two had taken up housekeeping in Jessica's Dallas apartment, and it looked to be a permanent arrangement. Charlie was in Virginia at the moment, closing on the sale of his house in Alexandria, so Jessica was all alone for a week or so.

I don't think anything is likely to come of this, Brad's the best tactician I ever met, and he's not the type to get in over his head. If it looks like it will turn out to be something, he'll send for help. Still, it wouldn't hurt to give Jess a call and a head's up just in case.

Besides, she's probably bored to tears sitting in that apartment all by herself waiting for Charlie to come home. If Willona and I didn't have so much going on right now I'd be bored spitless. Maybe she'll consider coming out here to spend the day with us. I think I will give her a call.

* * *

William Darnell Duckworth IV, "Bill" to his very few friends, CEO of Duckworth International Petroleum, had proven more than willing to dispatch his Gulfstream G650 to Pinedale, no questions asked. In his words, Brad 'could have anything he asked for.' Team Dallas had rescued him from captivity on the Island of Borneo, a tidbit that Fly found intriguing but knew nothing about. Duckworth's private office number had been in the directory on Brad's computer under 'Air Charter, Bill,' so Fly had called him. She, of course, had known who Bill Duckworth was, but she had not expected *him* to be the 'Bill' in the directory. Her admiration for Brad went up another notch. He had some interesting friends.

Fly had loaded the equipment container in the back of her new Ford pickup truck, not without some difficulty, the bag was heavy as hell, and managed to leave the ranchette without arousing any curiosity. The trip to Dallas-Fort Worth International was about forty miles give or take, and she made it inside an hour. A uniformed pilot met her at the Duckworth International Petroleum private hangar and had taken the heavy equipment bag without asking what was in it.

"You know where you're taking this?"

"Ralph Wenz Field Airport, Pinedale, Wyoming, ma'am. Mr. Duckworth gave me my instructions personally."

"He tell you who to give it to?"

"He said we would receive those instructions in flight, ma'am."

"Good enough." She wanted to tell him how important the delivery was, but she decided it would be better not to arouse his curiosity any more than it already was. As she drove back to the ranchette, she used her Bluetooth to call Jim Clancy in Denver, but her call went straight to voicemail. She left a message for him to call her back and then began composing a story to tell Vicky and Willona if they wanted to know where she had been.

* * *

"Are you sure he said Nicholas Ainsley?"

"No doubt about that, Jess, Fly was very sure."

"I can't imagine what a tech tycoon would be doing way the hell off in Wyoming, of all places. From what Brad told me, I don't even think they have electricity out where he was headed."

"Different strokes for different folks I guess. Who knows what goes on in the minds of men? If I wanted some time to rest and relax I'd head for someplace with a spa so I could be pampered and waited on hand and foot."

Jessica laughed. "I like camping and fishing, but I'd probably pick the spa too."

Vicky caught the flash of a brand-new red Ford pickup as it cruised past the kitchen window, headed for the barn. "Wonder where Fly went? She was in Brad's new comm center earlier. I didn't even know she left."

"No telling. She's been awfully busy out there the last couple of weeks. I'm glad Brad talked her into joining the team. Those gadgets of hers sure made a difference in El Salvador. We would have been in a world of hurt without them."

"I love the drones and the earwigs, but what amazed me is how she got access to those satellites."

Jessica's face took on a pensive look. "Things have sure changed a lot since we went to Alaska. Sometimes I feel like we're living in a science fiction movie."

"Me too."

* * *

Safely back in the barn, Fly spoke with the foremen of the carpentry and electrician crews and then closed herself inside the cubbyhole office she had appropriated for herself. She booted up her laptop and established a remote control link with her own lab at home and then began a search for satellite coverage of the Wind River region.

Weather and geostationary communications satellites were available, but they didn't have the thermal imaging capability she so desperately wanted. Fuming, she focused instead on creating a search program that would alert her to any reference to Taggart, the Denver FBI Field Office, Wyoming state and local law enforcement, and Nicholas Ainsley. After debugging the program, she stopped and researched the names of the prisoners who had escaped with Taggart at the Denver Airport. She added them to the search parameters. Within seconds of activating the search she began to get results.

Within an hour she was reaching for her sat phone and punching in Brad's number. The only response she got was a recorded message that his number was not in service at this time. Worried, she went to the microwave to heat some water for more of Jared's cocoa. She was sprinkling the powder over the water just as Jared had showed her to when she made up her mind. It was time to fess up to Vicky. She had a premonition that Brad had unknowingly bitten off more than he'd be able to chew, even with Ving and Jared to help him.

* * *

"You think Taggart has more men with him than the ones Brad saw chasing Ainsley?" Vicky was pacing back and forth in the small office and Jessica was leaning against the desk with her arms folded across her chest, frowning in concentration.

"I can't be certain, but I've collected a great deal of information in the last couple of hours that strongly suggests that is a possibility."

"Don't you have any of those magic high-tech gadgets that can confirm or disprove it?" Jessica asked.

"I am using a service called 'SecureWatch', but I'm having a little trouble logging into the more sensitive programs used by the military for real-time battlefield image resolution. Somebody at DoD (Department of Defense) has changed the passwords and they use the Advanced Encryption Standard (AES), a symmetric encryption algorithm that is one of the most secure on Earth. The U.S. Government uses it to protect classified information. Even if I had access to a Cray Supercomputer it could take a long time to crack it. I do have access to geospatial still imagery, but it takes forty-eight hours after the imagery is captured to show up online, so it will be late tomorrow before I can get anything useful."

"I'm not sure I understood all that, Fly, but what I got from it is that we're totally in the dark and there's nothing we can do about it…"

"Until tomorrow night, Vicky, unless my mainframe manages to decrypt the DoD passwords … and even then there's no guarantee one of the satellites in their network will be in orbit above Pinedale."

"In other words," Jessica said tightly, "we're screwed."

"Only for—" Fly glanced down at her old Timex wristwatch "—about thirty more hours."

"Thirty hours can be a lifetime, Fly."

"I know, Vicky, but I'm pulling up stills of the area for the latest seventy-two-hour period that are available online right now. It's a big area, and I had to request coverage for a twenty-square-mile sector because I have no idea where Taggart and his crew are holed up, and that's a *lot* of images. It's going to take a lot of work and just as much luck to locate them, but it's all I have to work with till the new stuff becomes available."

"Anything we can do to help?" Jessica was action oriented, and she was itching to be doing something ... anything.

"I can do what needs to be done faster by myself, Jessica. If you want to help, find a topographical map and see if you can find a likely place for a man on the run to hole up for a while. I know that's a stretch, but it's all I've got right now."

* * *

"Blue Team, go!" Special Agent in Charge (SAC) Lawrence Raines barked into his comm set. The word had come down from the hostage negotiator that all attempts to negotiate a deal with the leader of the group calling themselves Omega Three had failed. The group had taken over an entire three-story office building on the outskirts of Salt Lake City, holding twenty-six employees hostage.

The demands had been impossible; the release of four terrorist leaders being held at Gitmo, and Omega Three had refused to negotiate a good faith release of the hostages. The on-site FBI profiler's opinion was that Omega Three's threat to begin executing the hostages was real—and imminent—and that was enough for Raines to make the decision to start the rescue op. The situation was hairy, but he had faith in his team. That didn't keep him from worrying, but he was a consummate professional and he set his worries aside.

The internal count sequence started on the word 'Go!' and the op started to go down by the numbers. All five entrances to the building were breeched simultaneously, the front with small breeching charges followed by the tossing in of a flash bang. The others were nearly silent, three doors opened with breeching bars. The last, closest to the staircase leading to the third floor where the hostages were being held, was breeched with the aid of a portable plasma cutter.

As intended, Omega Three responded to the loudest and most obvious of the penetrations. Hostage Rescue Team (HRT) members in full body armor and carrying bulletproof shields returned fire with their suppressed H&K MP5s. Other members entered as silently as possible and made for the third floor. They were keyed up, highly strung professionals who endured the interminable negotiations as calmly as they could. When the op was concluded, they would crash, and crash hard. High-tension ops were draining to say the least, and this one definitely qualified as high tension. Most of the employees were female, very young or eligible for retirement. Little sisters and grandmas.

The conclusion was almost anti-climactic. The five members of Omega Three that survived had thrown down their weapons and surrendered after Raines personally took down their leader, Rasheed Al-Wazari (aka Eldon P. Marsh, who had converted to Islam while incarcerated at Utah State Prison), with a head shot. None of the little sisters or grandmas sustained an injury.

The debriefing, as usual, was nerve-racking and time-consuming. When it was over, Raines treated his men to dinner and released them to their hotel rooms. He, keyed up and wide awake despite his exhaustion, stayed up to write in his journal.

CHAPTER EIGHT

Day Two, 0637 hours

It was cold, and three hours sleep on the rocky ground had left all of them aching and miserable. Even so, "sleep is a weapon" was an axiom that had been hammered into them from their earliest days in the Corps, and experience had proven the value of that little tidbit of information time and again.

Brad suppressed a groan as he moved into a squatting position over the hole he had scooped in the ground the night before and began to heat water in his canteen cup for coffee. As he waited for the water to heat, he chewed thoughtfully on a Slim Jim and allowed his eyes to roam over the mountains around him. He had not appreciated just how high they were when they'd stopped the night before.

"Man, I am not lookin forward ta climbin' any a them today." Ving, sitting cross-legged in front of his own makeshift stove, was gnawing on some of the cold bacon he had snatched up from his griddle the day before and stuffed into a Ziploc bag while his own coffee water was heating.

Jared, whose cocoa was already hot because he had awakened first, sipped from his cup. "You gonna call Fly, Brad?"

"No. I want to get a location on Taggart and company first. I don't know how much charge is left in this battery, and I have to make sure I can use it for the airdrop."

"You gotta tell her where we are so she will know where ta drop it, Brad."

"I know that, Ving, but there's no telling where we'll be when it comes time to make the drop. I don't want to jump Taggart without knowing what he's going to throw at us first. We've got time…"

Jared cradled his cup in his hands.

"Yeah, but does Ainsley?"

Brad looked back at the forbidding mountain terrain. "We can't do him any good at all if we're dead."

Neither Ving nor Jared had a response to that. Five minutes later, they were on the trail hoofing it once more, Jared in the lead, Brad and Ving spread out about five meters behind him, constantly scanning the ground to either side looking for discards or signs of passage, and looking ahead for any signs of Taggart and his thugs. They were moving much faster today, not having to stop to make the cairns for Jared.

"She already sent the weapons, right?"

"Yes Ving, she's sending them to a bush pilot at Ralph Wenz Field outside of Pinedale. A jet would be too loud and it would have to drop the bag from too great an altitude."

"Wish you'd a told her ta send more bacon," Ving grumbled. "I'm gonna be eatin' that nasty jerky before ya know it." He held up the Ziploc bag containing the last of the bacon he'd cooked before leaving their camp, his face a caricature of pure unhappiness. "Man ought not ta haveta suffer that kinda deprivation, Brad, it just ain't civilized!"

It was impossible not to smile when Ving was in 'baconater' mode.

As Brad had feared, the trail began to wind up the mountain slope, the scree slippery and treacherous underfoot.

Jared raised a hand and then knelt down by what looked like a piece of khaki colored cloth.

"Looks like Ainsley is losing a lot of blood. Got an Ace bandage with a bloody gauze compress here." He looked a little to the side and saw the clear plastic wrapper for an Ace bandage with the packaging for a fresh compress tucked inside. The plastic had been half hidden by the scree. "Looks like they changed the dressing."

"They want him alive," Brad muttered hopefully.

"Looks like it. At least we know they ain't gonna let him bleed to death…"

"Leastways, not until they get what they want from him." Ving spat, as if to get a bad taste out of his mouth.

"He's been bleedin' pretty bad," Jared remarked. "That much blood loss an' he's gonna have a hard time fightin' off hypothermia."

"I think they'll find a way to keep him alive for the time being. Taggart knows he's rich as hell, and he's smart enough to know Ainsley's company's going to want some proof that he's still alive. I don't expect Taggart is going to let his paycheck die on him."

"I wouldn't count on that, Brad. That sonofabitch is capable of anything." Jared's lips pressed together in a thin, hard line. "We need to get movin' again." He kicked the bandage with the toe of his boot. "I'm not as sure as you are that Ainsley is still kickin'." He moved ahead, at a faster pace now, as if making up for the time they had spent with the bloody bandage. They had been following the faint trail all day, and it had been easier to follow as they moved along because Ainsley was obviously bleeding more heavily.

The blood trail was harder to follow now, probably because of the fresh dressing, but Jared moved steadily forward. They were moving more uphill now, the slope was steeper and harder to negotiate, but Jared was relentless. The pace he set never slackened, if anything it got faster. His Sharps was no longer slung across his back, he carried the heavy rifle at port arms, and he had a round chambered in the big single shot breech loader.

Trusting Jared's instincts, Brad unslung his Weatherby and chambered a round, the nine-lug bolt making its distinctive 'click' as they locked in place. Ving did the same with his Remington.

"I don't see nothin', I just got a feelin' we're getting' close," Jared called back over his shoulder. His eyes were scanning far ahead of them now. They could see the snow line far up ahead, but the scree had given way to high altitude native grass and wildflowers. Beyond that the mountains were bare but for the snow.

There were copses of trees, pine and cedar, scattered below the tree line, and it was these that Jared was looking at. He slowed down.

"Spread out. I feel like somebody's watchin' us."

* * *

They were supposed to be on lookout, but there wasn't anybody way the hell up there, hell, all they had seen in a couple of weeks was some elk, fox, jackrabbit and squirrels ... unless you counted that raggedy looking yahoo Jeffries and Jones had dragged in last night. Expensive clothes but tore up. They were leaning back against the whitebark pine tree, whittling, daydreaming, and thinking about the beer back in camp.

"What are you gonna do with your share of the money?" Randy Acres was whittling with the Kabar he had taken with him when he'd deserted. The Corps had wanted to send him back to Camp Shorabak, in Helmand province, home of the Afghan army's 215th Corps and including the adjoining American garrison of a couple hundred Marine advisers with Task Force Southwest. He'd had all the Taliban he wanted, thank you very much, and he'd waited till lights out one night just before deployment and headed for the mountains. He'd heard it through the grapevine that a renegade gunny was looking for help up near Pinedale and he'd been curious ... and here he was.

"You really think Taggart is gonna share with us, Acres?" Norm Coates glanced over at the nineteen-year-old deserter with an amused look on his face. "You musta been smokin' some a that jimson weed. He'll pay us, an' prolly pretty good, but you won't be getting' no big green."

Coates was from North Carolina, and he had escaped from the brig at LeJeune while on a work detail. He had run fast and far, and when he got tired of running, he'd found himself in Pinedale, Wyoming. He'd liked the homey feel of the mountains and decided to stay. Taggart and he had bumped into each other at the outpost store and one thing had led to another. Now he was back pulling boring ass guard duty again, but this time there was no corporal of the guard to give him a ration of shit for not being alert or for being out of uniform. The only real drawback was having to put up with this goofy jerk Acres.

"Yeah," Acres drawled, "but how *much* do you think he's gonna pay? I hear that guy they brought in is *mega* rich."

"Oh, he's rich as King Midas, an' I bet his company will pay millions for him ... but don't count on Taggart givin' us a fair share. We'll be lucky ta git 'nuff ta git outta here an' live like civilized people." He closed his eyes. "Hot showers, clean sheets, real food that ain't cooked by that fat little Puerto Rican..."

Acres grinned. "Hot and cold running pussy, man, and a new car, a Mustang maybe..."

"You're dreamin'."

Acres shoved his Kabar back into its sheath and rolled over on his stomach, cradling his M-16 in his arms. "Ain't nothing wrong with dreaming, pal."

I ain't your pal. I may jus' be a ol' country boy, but I'm smart 'nuff ta know not ta go 'round talkin' 'bout how much Taggart is gonna give us outta whatever he scores. That Taggart, he's a crazy man, I kin see it in his eyes. He'd kill ya soon as look at ya. All I want outta this is enough cash ta git back to some real mountains, ones that ain't covered with snow all year round. Ones that got grass an' flowers ever'where an' where people live ... not too close by but close 'nuff where ya kin visit when you've a mind to.

Coates rolled over and glanced down at the meadow below so he didn't have to look at the rocky, snow-covered peaks behind them. Pretty but sterile and boring. His eyes widened.

"Well, will ya lookit that!" he exclaimed. Three guys, looked like hunters, were spread out in a vee, walking up the slope real slow, like they were tracking elk. They were too far away for him to tell if they were walking toward the camp. They looked harmless to him. Those weren't military type guns, and the guys didn't look like cops...

The sudden sound of an M-16 going off right in his ear scared the hell out of him and then pissed him off.

"For fuck's sake, Acres! Have ya lost yer mind?" He threw his arm across the smoking barrel of the M-16 and shoved the muzzle into the ground. "Nobody said anything 'bout *shootin'* nobody! All we're s'posed ta do is let Taggart know if we see cops or soldiers comin'. Jeez..."

"Aww, I was just havin' a little fun. They might have been heading for the camp. I just wanted to scare 'em off.

"They ain't the Taliban, fuckhead, and if they *are* cops or soldiers, you just told 'em where we are. Jesus!" Coates peered around the trunk of the tree, watching as the three men scattered and ran. Something about the way they moved bothered him ... he had seen it before.

"We gonna be in the shit for sure if Jeffries heard that shot dude, an' I ain't takin the blame for it!" Coates was worried, and the look on Acres' face told him the kid had just now figured out he might be in deep shit. What kind of morons were they taking in the Corps these days? Hard to believe Acres had managed to survive a tour in Afghanistan.

Coates watched until the three hunters, which had to be what they were, had disappeared from sight. He hadn't seen where they had gotten off to, but he doubted they were going to come back. *Damn Acres!* Now they had to wait and see if anyone at the camp had heard the shot...

* * *

The shot rang out, and a split second later the bullet had struck a stone right next to Jared's foot and the ricochet whined off into the meadow. There was no cover in the meadow at all, so Jared crouched over as close to the ground as he could and began to run, darting off in different directions, zigzagging his way to the nearest copse of pines.

Brad and Ving did the same thing, making themselves as small a target as possible and making abrupt changes in direction so the shooter couldn't draw a bead on them. They reached the pines just seconds after Jared and took up defensive positions facing in the direction from which the shot had been fired.

"You see him?"

"No Brad, I never even saw the muzzle flash."

"I think it came from that grove up there," Ving said breathlessly.

"Sounded like an M-16, but the range is too far."

"He missed, that's all I care about." Jared was adjusting the Vernier sights on the Sharps, estimating the range to the pines and searching for any sign of movement.

Brad took in their surroundings. "If they come after us, we're going to have to pick off as many as we can while they're in the open. There's no cover anywhere near us. If he's got a crew of any size, we're screwed."

"Maybe they thought we was hunters or somethin'," Ving said. "All they coulda seen was assholes an' elbows..."

"Maybe they won't come after us, but I wouldn't count on it. Even if they don't we're stuck here till dark. I think we'll be able to follow that crease in the meadow, keeping these trees between us and them come nightfall."

"I don't want to get away," Brad said grimly. "I think tonight will be a fine time to run a recon." He pulled out the satellite phone.

CHAPTER NINE

Day Two, 1604 hours

"Stubborn man! Why hasn't he called?"

"I'm sure he has his reasons, Fly. Brad's a very level-headed guy." Vicky was trying to be reassuring, but she was worried. They still had no idea how many men Taggart might have with him.

"I'm not so sure everything's okay, Vicky." Jessica's face was pinched looking, concern written plainly all over it. "It's not like Brad to say he's going to do something and not do it. He's got to know we're worried…"

Vicky crossed over and wrapped an arm around Jessica's shoulder. "Brad is the most resourceful man I've ever met, and Ving and Jared are both extraordinary men. I believe in them, Jess."

"Brad's a legend in the Special Ops community, Jessica. I've been hearing stories about his accomplishments for years, even before he got out of the Corps." There was genuine respect and admiration in Fly's voice, though she was frowning in concentration as she reviewed the satellite stills on her computer monitor.

"I don't like this," she muttered to herself.

"What's up?" Vicky was beside the tech guru in a flash, Jessica right beside her.

"I've got some hot spots here, half a dozen of them." She pointed her finger at some blobs on the infrared images. "This is about twelve miles from where Brad and the guys were when we talked. I can't be certain..."

"What?" Jessica's voice had a quiver in it. "You can't be certain of what?"

Fly rolled her desk chair back and gave her a stern look. "I can't be certain of anything right now, Jess.

These are twelve miles from Brad's last known position. These are infrared stills from geological survey satellites with a resolution nowhere near as accurate as the military ones. I don't know if these spots represent fires or clusters of people. For all I know this could be a herd of elk."

"But you don't think that, do you?" Vicky prompted.

"No, I don't." Fly sighed. "See this brightest one here?" Her finger pointed to the brightest of the spots. "If I had to guess, I'd say that is a campfire, maybe a bonfire. These other spots"—she indicated a rough semicircle of faint glimmers around the most intense one—"I can't tell if they are smaller fires or clusters of people."

"You think it's Taggart and his men?"

Fly shook her head. "Vicky, there's no way for me to tell for sure until I get into one of the higher resolution feeds." She rested her chin on one slender hand, her elbow resting on the desk next to her laptop.

"Come on, Fly," Jessica urged. "You've been doing this for years, give us an educated guess."

A flash of annoyance crossed Fly's aristocratic face, her temper flaring, but she quickly got herself back under control. "Jessica, we're dealing in probabilities here, I can't give you a definitive answer. I can say with one hundred percent surety that there is *something* located about twelve miles north-northwest of the last location I got from Brad's sat phone, several somethings that have heat signatures I have no way to identify." She took a sip from her cup of cocoa.

"I can tell you that Brad reported seeing six men on the north side of the lake he was fishing at, but that was yesterday and these images were taken before Brad, Ving, and Jared even got there. But I can't tell you with any degree of certainty if this could be Taggart's camp or not." She fixed Jessica with a steady look, her expressive brown eyes sympathetic.

"I can also tell you that this image covers an area at a much higher elevation than the one at Brad's campsite, very near the snowline ... which seems to me to be an odd place to put a campsite because it would be pretty cold there." Awkward silence enveloped the little office space, none of them sure what to say.

* * *

"I didn't mean to aggravate her." Jessica sat at the kitchen table, picking at a lettuce, tomato, and onion salad with raspberry vinaigrette dressing she had made and subsequently lost her appetite for.

"She's worried about the boys, too, Jess..."

"You can't blame her, not after what she told us about that Taggart guy's background. That guy is seriously bad news." Fly had given them a complete rundown on Harlan Taggart, and what she had revealed about him had made her blood run cold. It bothered her even more to know that Brad had a history with the man. None of them knew that Jared had a history with him too.

"I've been reading about that place, Vicky, the Wind River Range. Did you know they've found ancient villages in those mountains? Ten thousand years ago people lived there. They found one in Dubois, not far from where Brad and the guys are, and they think there are more of them."

"I had no idea."

"Vicky, those bright spots Fly showed us, they were arranged kind of like a little village. You don't suppose…?"

"That Taggart somehow found one when he was running from the law and decided to set up housekeeping there? Really Jessica?"

"I know it sounds a little far-fetched…"

"A *little* far-fetched? It sounds like something out of a comic book!"

Jessica's lips tightened and pursed, and if Vicky hadn't known her so well she'd have sworn the woman was pouting.

"Well, *I* don't think it's *that* far-fetched. Taggart is on the run, not only is he an escapee and a murderer, he is a suspect in an armed robbery and the Feds are after him. If I was Taggart, I'd head for someplace as isolated and as far away from people as I could get. Those mountains fit the bill perfectly."

She wasn't pouting. Jessica *knew* something had gone badly awry, she just couldn't explain *how* she knew, and she was determined to do something about it with or without the help of Vicky and Fly. What to do? It had to be quick, which meant she'd get no help from Charlie, who was in Virginia, closing on his house in Alexandria. She smiled at the thought of Charlie. She had fallen for him hard on the mission to Alaska, and things had progressed to the point where they were considering making their arrangement permanent. That's why he was selling the house in Alexandria; they wanted to build a home together in Texas.

The other option was Pete Sabrowski, but he was in New Jersey with his son and grandsons, waiting on the arrival of his newest grandchild. It had been a long time since Pete had seen his son, and, besides, Jessica suspected there would not be time for him to return before she had to take action. No, she had to do something even if it meant she had to do it alone. Without saying another word, she rose and headed for the armory. She had her own keys.

* * *

The newest images had just come in, and though they were of a better resolution, they did not cover the coordinates where she had seen what she'd suspected were fires. She remonstrated with herself. Long years' experience as an Intelligence analyst told her that the spots *were* either fires or clusters of human bodies (or both) and she had deliberately withheld her opinion. It was entirely likely that she could count on Vicky to keep her head, but Jessica was younger, and she was impulsive. As far as Fly was concerned, the last thing in the world Brad needed was for Jessica to go off half-cocked and get herself in trouble ... or worse.

The good news was that she had a clearly resolved thermal image of Brad, Ving, and Jared around a campfire in exactly the same coordinates that had been on his sat phone when he'd called, though the image had been taken before the call. She consoled herself with the fact that more images were uploading to the SecureWatch site as she sat there.

The images from this particular satellite were far clearer, and it would probably be less than an hour before she could download them.

Easy girl! You're jumping the gun, aren't you? There may be people at that site, but you have no concrete evidence that they aren't a group of survivalists or even Boy Scouts for Pete's sake! Patience! There may come a time when you have to make assumptions but not now.

Fly drummed her fingertips on the desktop, waiting for the images. Then she made another cup of Jared's cocoa, the last of his makin's. It really was the best she'd ever tasted. She took a sip. The cayenne pepper in the mix definitely added something special to the mix, but there was something more, something she couldn't put her finger on.

Setting the mug down abruptly, she picked her cell phone up off the desk and dialed Jim Clancy's number. He answered on the first ring.

"Fly, is that you?"

"Yeah Jim, give me an update on your armored car heist." There was a hesitant silence on Clancy's end.

"Fly, I could get in serious trouble ... it's an ongoing investigation..."

"Tell me, Clancy, or I'll tell your wife about your penchant for candy cigarettes." Clancy had tried, unsuccessfully, to quit smoking during an investigation into an ISIS sleeper cell in Manassas, Virginia, and had spent several days in a motel room filled with electronic surveillance gear ... with Fly as a partner. He had bought a case of candy cigarettes and had gone through them in a day and a half and then had to sneak out of the motel room to buy more because he didn't want the rest of his FBI team to know about it. They had laughed about the episode many times over the intervening years, but Fly had never told anyone else.

"Okay. We've got confirmation that Taggart was the perp, and he had seven other prisoners with him when he did it. I don't have the names with me right now, but I remember Jeffries, Coates, Acres, and a former medical corpsman named Jones."

"Any idea where they're headed?"

"I swear, Fly, I don't know. The team is running down leads. Memphis, Baton Rouge, even Kansas City." He paused, as if he was short of breath. "I gotta go, Fly. The SSAC (Supervisory Special Agent in Charge) is riding my ass about this case and I've got to be in a briefing... Oh jeez, I shoulda been there three minutes ago! Bye Fly!" He was gone.

Fly set the cell phone down beside her laptop and pursed her lips thoughtfully. Eight men instead of five, and Taggart had had three weeks and a buttload of money to spend. He could be anywhere ... or he could have bought himself some weapons and men and holed up in some isolated spot till the heat was off. Spotting a target of opportunity like

Nicholas Ainsley would have given a man like Taggart wet dreams, and a whole world of possibilities would have tempted him. A quick, easy score. She turned back to the laptop, waiting impatiently for the requested images to download.

Day Two, 1723 hours

Senior Game Warden Dalton Herring winced at the sight before him and dismounted his horse. He'd been going to stop by the outpost store to grab a cup of coffee on his way back to the line shack he was staying in for a few days while he checked out rumors of a gang of poachers who had reportedly killed a cow elk and skinned it. The guy who'd reported it had not been able to give more than a vague description of where he'd found it, but he'd produced an ear tag, still attached to the ear, as proof. He'd also taken a picture of the offal left behind by the poachers, which had given Herring an idea where to look.

He hadn't found the elk, but what he *had* found sickened him. It was a man, indeterminate age and hair color... There wasn't much of his face left and his hair, which was a tad longish, was so bloody that Herring couldn't make out the color in the rapidly diminishing daylight. Putting on a pair of latex gloves he'd taken from his saddlebags, he knelt down and patted down the body, careful not to disturb anything.

The Wyoming Highway Patrol was kind of sticky about anybody, including game wardens, contaminating their crime scenes, and this one certainly qualified as a crime scene. He found a wallet and painstakingly pulled it out of the man's pocket before backing away and standing beside his horse.

Opening the wallet, he found a California driver's license and reached for the portable radio on his belt.

"Herring to base."

"This is base, go ahead, Dalton."

"Need you to run a California DL for me. Perry, Simon D. Subject is a white male, D.O.B. 10/2/1985."

"You stoppin' traffic violators on horseback these days, Dalton?" The operator sounded amused.

"Not today, Sandy. This one is deceased. Looks like I'm gonna need you to notify the Highway Patrol. The County won't even come out this far."

There was total silence for a moment as the dispatcher suddenly realized that a recording of this conversation was likely to be played in a court of law.

"Roger that, Herring. Stand by."

* * *

I've never jumped an equipment bag before, but I've seen videos on the internet and I've watched the guys do it half a dozen times now. The hardest part is remembering to release the lowering line and making sure I have the chute headed upwind. That would be harder with a standard chute, but I'll be jumping one of the ram-air chutes so that won't be a problem. The question is, what am I going to need to take with me? What would Brad take?

She settled on the standard M-16 rather than the CAR-4 she usually carried because of the range involved in the terrain she was heading for. The '16 had a slight range advantage over the shorter CAR-4. Jared had his heavy old Sharps, but to hear him tell it, he'd rather use that than the Barret he had stashed in the rack.

What did Fly send him? How can I make a decision about what I need to take if she doesn't tell me what she sent? If I ask her, she's going to tell Vicky what I'm planning and they'll gang up on me. Crap!

Squatting down on the concrete floor of the armory, she put her head in her hands and fought back tears of frustration. Brad was in trouble, she could *feel* it, but she was stymied by things she had absolutely no control over.

* * *

The latest images began to download, and Fly's attention was riveted on the laptop monitor. The one she wanted, the one she had been waiting for, flashed onto the screen and she immediately sent it to the seventy-two-inch high definition television screen the electricians had hooked up for her earlier in the day. The carpenters had completed the temporary cabinet for her the day before yesterday.

The picture was detailed, but the resolution of the satellite image was still not as fine as the ones from military satellites. It *was* fine enough to show that the bright spots she had seen earlier were individual campfires, but it did not dissolve individual human bodies. She felt a chill. She couldn't get an accurate count, but there were people clustered around the fires. A *lot* more people than she had figured on.

There was still no way to determine whether the people were Taggart's band or not, but she had a bad feeling in her gut. Should she tell Vicky?

While she was trying to decide, the search program window from what she now called 'The Taggart Search' popped up onscreen. It was a preliminary incident report from a game warden originating from Pinedale, Wyoming. A body had been found a few miles from the outpost store near the guys' camp. Identity of the body was being withheld pending an investigation by the Wyoming Highway Patrol. It was all circumstantial, possibly coincidence, but the evidence was piling up and it was beginning to give her some serious doubts about whether she had done the right thing by holding back on Vicky and Jessica. Jessica in particular was going to be difficult, but she had to be told anyway. It just wasn't going to be pleasant. Damn Brad for not turning on his sat phone! She needed to know what he wanted her to do.

Day Two, 1943 hours

"Where's Jessica? She needs to hear this and I'd really rather not have to say it twice."

"I texted her after you texted me. She'll be along in a minute." Vicky cocked one hip to the side and fixed Fly with an inquisitive stare. "What's up?"

Fly glanced at the door, hoping that Jessica would come on. She'd meant what she said when she told Vicky she didn't want to have to repeat herself, but she didn't want to annoy the woman either. She was saved by Jessica's breathless appearance.

"Did you hear from him?"

"No, but I've got more information that I thought you should have."

"Soooo, go ahead…" Jessica stood in the doorway, hands on her hips, glaring at Fly.

Fly punched up the image again, and it opened on the big television screen. "This image has a better resolution than the last one, but I still can't tell you how many people are in the camp … and I can't say for certain who they are or what they are doing."

Jessica's expression was one of alarm. "There are more than just eight people there!"

"It sure looks like it," Vicky said. She hadn't moved, but her eyes were focused on the big screen.

"But keep in mind we still don't have a positive I.D. on these guys. They could be anybody."

"Yeah, including Taggart," Jessica muttered.

Fly sighed audibly. "There's more…"

"Go ahead," Vicky was facing her now, expressionless.

"Just before I texted you, I got a report from a search program I set up earlier today. It finds and selects anything remotely related to the keywords I plugged into the search parameters. I printed it out for you." She lifted two sheets of paper from the output tray of her printer and handed one each to Vicky and Jessica. "I'm afraid this is a little more unsettling than the satellite images."

"Oh my God!" Jessica staggered but pulled herself together quickly. Before she could speak, Vicky had wadded up her copy and shoved it in her pocket.

"We need to get to the armory, Jessica." She was moving past Jessica and out the door of the office before Fly could protest.

"We still don't know where to drop the equip..." But her words fell on deaf ears. Vicky and Jessica were already gone.

* * *

As long as Jessica's legs were, Vicky's were longer, and she walked *fast*. Jessica had to struggle to keep up. Conversation was out of the question.

"You got your keys to the armory?" Vicky asked, stopping and turning around halfway to the concrete building beside the barn.

"Yeah," Jessica gasped, embarrassed to be out of breath so quickly. Vicky's mad dash out of Fly's office had caught her by surprise. "I was out here when you texted me, that's why it took me so long to get there." She'd had to fumble with her key ring to find the keys to the three separate deadbolt locks on the steel door.

Vicky was moving again and not speaking. She stopped at the door and held her hand out for Jessica's keys. Jessica noticed that she had no trouble recognizing the keys and which locks they fit. She made a mental note to become more familiar with the keys.

Vicky stepped inside and looked at the heavy equipment bag and the parachute sitting side by side on the concrete floor.

"You figured on going without me?"

"I didn't think you would agree to go with me."

"I haven't agreed to go at all," Vicky said calmly. "We still need the coordinates where Brad wants the stuff Fly already sent and we haven't got confirmation on the identity of the group at the camp."

"But—"

"What all did you put in the bag?"

Jessica told her.

"We need more, Jess. And for your information, when you go, and I believe you will, I'm going with you." Her tone brooked no argument, and Jessica moved to open the heavy equipment bag. There was still a lot of room inside it.

Vicky walked over to the rack where the 'chutes were stored and lifted out her own ram-air parachute, carrying it over to where Jessica was standing, and set it down by the first chute. She didn't ask Jessica to hand her M-16 over from the rack. Vicky had her own personal M-16, already zeroed at two hundred and fifty meters, and it had her initials scratched in the barrel.

She opened the extractor cover and shoved her thumb into the chamber, thumbnail up, and looked down the bore to check for dust. Satisfied that the bore was spotless, she set the rifle in the equipment bag and strode over to the ammo barrel. Grabbing an empty Claymore bag, she stuffed nine fully charged thirty-round magazines into it. She hesitated a moment then grabbed three more magazines out of the barrel and then carried the bag and extra magazines over to the O.D. green equipment bag and set them carefully inside.

"M-79," she snapped, holding her hand out.

Jessica rushed to the rack and snatched the short, stubby grenade launcher out of its spot. She handed it to Vicky and didn't wait to be asked. The crate of M-79 rounds was right beside the launcher's rack.

"How many?"

"Give me a dozen; then keep four to go in your rucksack."

Jessica complied. It had not really occurred to her earlier to take the little grenade launcher along, it would have been added weight for her to carry alone.

"Vicky, when do we leave?"

Vicky rounded on her, green eyes smoldering. "We're not leaving yet, Jess. I want to go to Brad as badly as you do, but we can't do him any good wandering around those mountains looking for him. We have to know where he is first."

Jessica stared down at the boots on her feet, trying to conceal the emotions roiling inside of her. "What if he's hurt, Vicky? What if the battery is dead in his sat phone?" She scuffed at the floor with the toe of one boot.

"Then we'll leave as soon as Fly gets her real-time high resolution images and we will go to Wyoming." Her face was emotionless. "And heaven help that bastard if he's done anything to hurt our guys…"

Vicky's face became mobile again, as if verbalizing her intentions had somehow unlocked her normal personality. She reached into the heavy equipment bag and lifted out her M-16, handing it to Jessica.

"Here, put this back in the rack."

Jessica shot her a questioning look, but Vicky was busy reaching for an MK-46. The MK-46 is a variant of the M-249, developed for Special Operations forces. The design did away with the carrying handle and the tripod-mounting lug and added a magazine well to accept M16-style magazines as well as being capable of handling a disintegrating belt of 5.56 ammo. With its collapsible buttstock and fold-down bipod, the MK-46 is a light, compact, wicked instrument of destruction capable of firing seven hundred thirty rounds a minute at a maximum effective range of eight hundred meters.

Almost as an afterthought, she grabbed the two American 180 submachine guns Team Dallas had used so successfully in El Salvador. The deadly little American-180s, developed in the 1960s, fired .22 LR cartridges from a pan magazine at a rate of 1200 rounds per minute. When fired, they made a sound like a swarm of angry hornets, and the volume of fire was more than adequate to send even the most experienced of troops diving for cover.

Their standard pan magazines held one hundred and eighty .22 LR cartridges, but Jared had fitted them with aftermarket magazines that carried two hundred and seventy-five rounds and added flash suppressors to help break up the telltale muzzle flash that would give away the shooter's position. Short of carrying an actual mini-gun, the American 180s were the most effective suppressive fire weapons any of them had ever used.

Vicky grabbed a couple of the drum magazines and then, after a moment's hesitation about carrying the extra weight, she added four more to the bag. The bad thing about the little submachine guns was that they went through a great deal of ammo in a very short time. One thing was certain. Brad would be loaded for bear.

CHAPTER TEN

Day Two, 2117 hours

They had moved out as soon as the sun was completely down, mostly low crawling at a snail's pace because they had no idea where … or who … their shooters were. Jared had located them and signaled contact to Brad and Ving. With infinite patience he had closed to within ten meters of the copse and had laid, immobile, for over an hour watching the two men wearing a mix of military and civilian clothing. The M-16s they carried had thirty-round 'banana' magazines, and the way they were semi-concealed convinced Jared that these men had some kind of military background, and though they were obviously slackers, it was clear to him that they were supposed to be a listening post.

Patiently, he waited, listening and observing, until the two men were relieved by another pair of men.

The relief approached, talking quietly, their own M-16s slung carelessly over their shoulders. All four of them were taking their LP/OP duties very casually.

Unimpressed with their lack of professionalism, Jared crawled back to Brad and Ving and signaled for them to back off. He led them to a depression that offered the concealment afforded by a cluster of dog fennel and then began a terse, whispered estimate of the situation.

"I think we found 'em. Pretty sure it's some of Taggart's bunch. That's an LP/OP, but they're lazy. Relief just showed up, an' I'm thinkin' we can follow 'em back to their base camp when they get through jokin' and jawin'." His disdain for the guards was evident.

"Reckon why they didn't pursue us after they fired that shot?" Ving was puzzled.

"Lazy," Jared said quietly.

"I'm more curious about why nobody came to check on them after that," Brad muttered.

"I'm thinkin' Taggart has rounded up a bunch of losers, Brad. He wouldn't have set an LP/OP up if he didn't have enough extra people to do it."

"We need to know what we're up against, guys. I'm getting a bad feeling…"

"Their base camp can't be far. The relief came from upslope. I can follow 'em when they head back."

"*We* can follow them, Jared. When we see their camp, we'll need to do a recon. We need to do this slow and easy, guys. I want an in-depth evaluation of their strength and the camp layout. Then we need to back off far enough so I can call in the coordinates for the air drop." He knew the ordnance he had asked Fly for would already be waiting at the Ralph Wenz Field with the bush pilot, the woman was incredibly efficient.

* * *

Jared was right. The two men were lackadaisical as they strolled back toward their camp, which was upslope. The younger one carried his rifle cowboy style, one hand on the pistol grip, the forestock resting on his shoulder. They didn't appear to be in any hurry, and neither of them seemed to be much aware of their surroundings. Jared could tell that the older one didn't care at all for the younger man. They didn't talk to each other at all as they walked. That they were bored and that they were tired was evident in their posture and attitude.

Jared fell back, giving them plenty of space. He looked back to check on Brad and Ving, but they were well concealed. He got to his feet and into a half crouch. When the guards were far enough away that he could barely see them, he matched his pace to theirs and moved forward.

They had only traveled a hundred or so meters before he noticed a change in their posture. The two straightened up, and both moved their weapons to port arms—and that set off alarm bells in Jared's head. They were approaching a larger grove of trees, and he could see the flickering glow of firelight between the trunks.

Jared sank down in the shadow of a cedar tree, its low-hanging branches giving him a measure of concealment though it offered no cover. Keeping his eyes away from the flickering light, he began his visual assessment of the camp, searching every inch of it as thoroughly as he could. Irritated, he saw that he could not conduct the reconnaissance on his own, as he had hoped. He backed out from beneath the branches of the cedar and slowly made his way back to Brad and Ving, who had taken up concealed positions so well that he almost low crawled past Ving. He waved at him, got the big man's attention, and then crawled off, away from the camp.

* * *

"I saw three GP Mediums, each one surrounded by a low wall of stones ... bigger than the ones in the scree downslope."

"They haven't had time."

"I don't think they built those walls from scratch, Brad. Looks like some kinda old settlement, like really old."

"Three GP Mediums will hold a lotta guys," Ving mumbled.

"We've got to get better intel."

"This place is sheltered, Brad. There's a cliff behind the camp, solid stone an' straight up. Whoever built this place was thinkin' 'defensive position' when he chose this spot."

"How high?" The moon was still mostly full, and if he could get a high enough vantage point, it was possible that he could get a more accurate count and, even more important, an idea of how

Taggart's crew was armed. Everything depended on the density of the canopy.

Brad did a quick mental review of the skillsets of Ving and Jared and came to a decision.

"Ving, you take the east side of the encampment. Focus on any defensive positions. I'll take the bluff. Jared, you take the west side. Hopefully you can locate Ainsley or at least locate where they're holding him. That and their numbers and weaponry are the most critical bits of information I need. I already don't care much for the odds, especially if we have to engage before we can get the ordnance drop. We'll do a three sixty recon, and then meet up at the military crest of that hillside to the east side. Any questions?" There were none. The three men faded noiselessly into the shadows.

* * *

Taggart was in a cranky mood. The shot from the LP/OP earlier had pissed him off mightily, and he'd had to struggle with himself to keep from going down there and going off on Coates and Acres. Coates was experienced enough to know better, and Acres was green despite his combat tour. Now, along with all the other details he was figuring out about the ransom for Ainsley, he had to worry about three hunters who had been scared shitless running off at the mouth. He wasn't as concerned about the body of Ainsley's companion. It might even be springtime before that body was discovered, if it ever was. There hadn't been time to go back and hide the body because they were chasing Ainsley.

Ainsley. That guy had surprised him, running for miles over rough terrain with a gimpy leg. They had finally caught him though. He'd put up a helluva fight for a computer geek, that was for sure, but the five of them had taken him down all right.

Taggart stood up so quickly that he startled Jeffries, who was sitting by the campfire with a beer in his hand.

"Easy on that stuff, Jeffries," he said, pointing at the beer. "Go get Ainsley and bring him out here. Tie him to that dead tree, an' then build a little fire in front of it. I got some questions for him an' I wanna be able to see his face good."

Jeffries dumped his beer, crushed the can, and slowly got up to walk over to the tent where Ainsley was being held. He was getting tired of Taggart's manner. The guy acted like he was still a gunny and this was still the Corps, and it was wearing on most of the guys. Taggart was leading through fear ... that and the promise of money. All of them had military experience, and most of them had been forced to deal with sadists like Taggart at one time or another. He opened the flap to the GP medium and stepped inside, blinking fast to adjust his eyes to the darkness.

"Get up!" he barked. "Get up!"

Ainsley's eyes popped open at the sound of Jeffries' voice. He'd been dozing fitfully. The ground was hard, and he'd only had his jacket to lie on. The corpsman had brought him a poncho to cover himself with, but the nylon garment had done little to warm him. His entire leg felt swollen and it ached. He wondered dispassionately if he was getting an infection. Byron and his blistered feet had slipped his mind completely.

"The boss wants to talk to you. C'mon, we're going outside."

Ainsley felt his arms being grabbed roughly, causing the handcuffs to bite painfully into his wrists, but he made no sound. When he was on his feet, Jeffries gave him a shove and he stumbled toward the open tent flap.

The air had a chill to it, but Ainsley breathed deeply, smelling the fragrance of pine and cedar, a huge change from the canvas odor inside the stuffy tent. He shivered. As cold as it had been in the tent, it was colder outside. Jeffries shoved him again, and he limped in the direction he had been pushed.

"Jeffries! Where are your manners? Set our guest down by this here dead tree an' let him rest!" Taggart looked around the camp, his eyes coming to rest on Acres, who was sitting in front of one of the GP Mediums drinking a beer. Acres, the yahoo that had taken a potshot at the hunters.

"Acres! Git over here an' build me a small fire," he bellowed. *I ain't forgettin' you prob'ly gave away our location, you scumbag. I found us the safest, most remote spot to hide out undetected for as long as we needed to an' you blew it 'cause you ain't got the sense of an earthworm!* The kid was a deserter, and Taggart had a low opinion of deserters, despite his own status as an escaped prisoner.

Acres got up resentfully and began to collect firewood, but he didn't set down his beer first. He had just finished an eight-hour detail at the LP/OP and he saw no reason why Taggart couldn't have picked one of the other guys for this shit detail. It wasn't fair!

Jeffries put his hand on Ainsley's shoulder and pushed him down into a sitting position with his back against the dead whitebark pine in the clearing that was near the center of the encampment. He took a short piece of nylon rope from around his waist and used it to secure Ainsley's cuffs to the tree and started to walk away.

"Damnit Jeffries! Post a guard on him!" Taggart roared. "Tell him to shoot this pissant if he gives him even a hint of trouble!"

Jeffries, pissed, crooked a finger at Coates, who'd been watching the whole episode from his place near the flap of the GP Medium he shared with nine other guys, got to his feet quickly. After a moment's hesitation, he reached down and picked up his M-16. He knew he was being singled out because of

Acres' fuck-up, and he was not happy, but he was smart enough not to let it show. Despite the laxness of a few of the others, Taggart ran a pretty tight military style organization, and he was volatile as hell when he was displeased.

He took up a spot next to the prisoner where the man could clearly see the rifle. And he seethed with anger inside. *Damn Acres!*

* * *

Brad peered down on the encampment through the forty-power Redfield Adjustable Ranging telescope on his Weatherby from a spot atop the bluff that gave him an incredibly clear view in the light of the waxing gibbous moon. The light gathering qualities of the scope were extraordinary.

Why Taggart had not posted a lookout on the bluff was a mystery to Brad. There were three visible GP Medium tents on what appeared to be the foundations of some ancient structures. To all appearances, the camp was set up on the ruins of some prehistoric village.

One GP Small was set up well away from the others ... he presumed that one belonged to Taggart. Oh yes, he had seen Taggart, and he had heard the bastard yelling at a couple of his troops, though he couldn't quite make out what he was saying. A second man, one he recognized as one of Ainsley's pursuers from the day before, got up from the largest campfire and crossed over to the southernmost GP Medium and came back out pushing a limping figure in front of him. Ainsley! He was still alive, but he looked a little worse for wear.

There were three camouflaged positions spread out across the southern edge of the crescent-shaped camp, and Brad felt his hackles rise when he recognized the distinctive barrel, carrying handle, and folding bipods of M-60 machine guns.

Where the hell did Taggart get those '60s? We don't have the firepower to take on three crew-served weapons! Hell, my Weatherby only holds three rounds, Jared's Sharps is a single-shot falling block breech loader, and I don't even know what Ving's Remington holds, but it can't be more than four rounds. We are flat outgunned! Shit!

He wanted to back off in a hurry. If something happened before they could collect the ordnance package he'd requested Fly send them they would be massacred. The smartest thing he could do at this point was back off and keep an eye on Taggart and call for whatever backup was available. That was not something he wanted to do, but he was no fool ... but first he needed to know what Ving and Jared had discovered.

Brad Jacobs had never backed down from a fight in his life, but he had never engaged a superior force unless he'd been left with no choice. It wasn't that he was afraid, he was not. What he was not willing to do was pit the two closest friends he'd ever had against insurmountable odds.

* * *

Jared slithered on his belly, utilizing every sliver of shadow and every scintilla of available cover to conceal himself. His movements were achingly slow, motion being the key component to detecting intruders at night. He was confident in his ability to move undetected. He had once almost been stepped on by a Taliban fighter who had stepped *over* his outstretched arm during a firefight in a wadi in Helmand Province.

Penetrating Taggart's camp had proven to be far easier. The men, though obviously well organized, were not as alert as they should have been, and all eyes were on the campfires instead of focusing outward as they should have been.

When he encountered the first crew-served weapon position, he froze until he realized that it was not manned. The fact that Taggart had crew-served weapons—further inspection revealed two more—curdled his stomach. For a second, he toyed with the idea of sabotaging the '60 he was next to, but he realized that his ego wanted to write a check his ass couldn't cash. The bolt on the M-60 weighed three pounds, and the chance of him making a discernible metal-on-metal noise when he tried to disable it was very nearly one hundred percent. He immediately quashed his impulse.

Moving forward at a pace slower than any snail's, he began to count warm bodies. When he reached the foot of the bluff, he had counted twenty-three men, excluding Taggart, and excluding Ainsley, who was tied to a dead whitebark pine near the center of the camp. Ainsley had a guard standing next to him, a guard armed with an M-16 pointed at his head. Taggart was standing in front of Ainsley, hands on his hips and a look of fury on his face. Ainsley was talking calmly, like a schoolteacher lecturing his class.

"I don't know who you are, mister, but I can tell you with absolute certainty that my company has security protocols in place that prohibit them from paying a ransom ... even for me. The only way you can get cash is if I call my head of security and give him a code word that only he and I know."

Taggart glared at him, his eyes bulging.

"You're a lying sonofabitch!" He had never trusted rich people. They were always out to screw the little guy. Always.

Ainsley, remarkably calm under the circumstances, responded coolly.

"I can give you his direct number. His name is Nolan Shepard, and he's head of my security." What Ainsley did *not* tell Taggart was that Shepard had a special phone that only he and Ainsley were privy to. That special phone had the ultra high-tech, and even more highly secret, technological capability of instantly tracing any call made to it in a matter of seconds rather than the normal three-minute tracing software. It could even access GPS positioning sensors, which *all* satellite phones possessed by law.

Taggart's fury got away from him then, and he lashed out with the toe of his boot, catching Ainsley on the jaw and rendering him unconscious.

"Jeffries!" Taggart yelled. "Shoot this man if he tries to get up!"

Jared's own jaw throbbed, and the veins at his temple stood out in high relief as he flashed back to the moment Taggart had done the same to him. It took every ounce of self-control he possessed not to unsling his Sharps and perforate Taggart's skull with a .52 caliber lead pill, but he managed. Taking Taggart out now, with his men all around him, would be suicidal ... and in all likelihood would get Ainsley killed. It was time to get the hell out of Dodge...

* * *

Despite his size, Ving was nearly as quiet as Jared in a recon. He had the almost magical ability to fade into invisibility in any environment ... a neat trick for a black man who weighed two hundred and sixty pounds. What he saw in Taggart's camp (he recognized the bastard too) was chilling. He didn't even have to think about it. Brad was going to have to call for reinforcements. Taggart's crew was too big to take on with three men, no matter what kind of ordnance Fly sent. Any kind of action the three of them could take that would neutralize Taggart's team was almost guaranteed to get Nicholas Ainsley DRT.

Day Two, 2247 hours

Brad waited in the spot he'd specified, at the military crest of the hill north-northwest of the encampment at the base of a lone whitebark pine. The battery indicator on his sat phone told him the power was almost gone, but he wasn't going to turn it on anyway until he had debriefed Ving and Jared. The three of them had stumbled onto a hornet's nest and if they weren't careful they were going to get Nicholas Ainsley killed ... not to mention bringing about their own demise.

He needed to gather as much information from Ving and Jared as he could, condense it into a short, definitive narrative, and relay it to Fly as succinctly as possible so that there could be no mistaking of any details. Most of all, he needed to make damned sure that Vicky and Jessica stayed in Dallas. Even if he could get reinforcements from law enforcement (at any level), this could get very hairy very quickly. He had no way of knowing that Vicky and Jessica were getting ready to board Duckworth's Gulfstream at Dallas-Fort Worth International Airport.

CHAPTER ELEVEN

Day Three, 0109 Hours

Vicky's cell phone rang while she and Jessica were waiting for Duckworth's Gulfstream to finish their preflight inspections. She turned her head to Jessica and spoke in a tense voice.

"It's Brad!"

Turning her face forward again, she pressed the telephone icon on the home screen of her phone and answered.

"Brad? Is everything okay? We've been worried to death!"

"I don't have much time, Vicky, so listen closely and I'll answer your questions later, okay?

She had no intention of interrupting him, but she already had a plan of action. She was willing to modify it, but she would be damned if she was going to let him shut her out of anything. "Okay."

"First, we have visual confirmation. All three of us have identified the man as Taggart. We know he has at least twenty-three, no, make that twenty-five men counting the two at their LP/OP and three crew-served weapons that we can verify. They have Ainsley tied to a tree trunk right now." He paused for breath.

"Jared heard Taggart order one of his men to shoot Ainsley at the first hint of trouble. Vicky, I don't know for certain if they intend to kill him or not, but the way Taggart was treating him doesn't bode well for his survival. My best guess is Taggart is going to try to get some ransom money for him ... and based on what I know of him, I'd be willing to bet Taggart is going to consider him a loose end and eliminate him once he has the cash in hand. Get hold of Fly and see if she can find any backup personnel close by. We need some heavy support, and we need it fast, but I don't want you to call in Pete. He couldn't get here from New Jersey soon enough to help any, and he has that new grandkid on the way."

"Brad, Fly's staying in the new comm center, I'll fill her in as soon as we're off the phone. She's been trying to access real-time satellite feed over your area, but the right kind of satellite won't be over the Wind River Range until sometime tomorrow ... make that today."

"Vicky, I don't have much time, the battery is failing on this phone. Listen to me... Under no circumstances do I want you or Jess to come up here, understand?"

"Give me your coordinates and a location where we can make the air drop, Brad," she answered, deliberately ignoring his demand. He did, and she repeated them aloud as she scribbled them on the back of a magazine from the table in the waiting area of the Duckworth private hangar.

"The ordnance you sent for should be with the bush pilot now, Brad. It will probably take at least a couple of hours to alert the guy and get him airborne and over your area."

"Belay that, Vicky. It's too damned quiet up here at night, and I don't want to alert Taggart that we're coming before we have to. Depending on what kind of help Fly can locate, belay that too. Give him instructions to make the drop at daybreak. We're going to have to engage Taggart about first light no matter what, and I'd rather not do that with this Weatherby."

"Brad—" She was about to argue with him about engaging Taggart without waiting for backup, but he broke in as she was trying to get the words out.

"I don't have time for this, Vicky, just *do* it!" The call ended abruptly, leaving Vicky fuming.

"What'd he say?" Jessica asked anxiously.

"No time," Vicky rasped, speed dialing Fly. "Just listen."

Fly answered before the first ring finished. "Yeah?"

Vicky rattled off the two sets of coordinates. "You get that?"

"Yeah," Fly replied, typing furiously.

"Don't call the bush pilot yet. Brad wants to wait for the drop until daybreak."

"He could have told me earlier," Fly grumbled. "Would have saved a ton of money."

"Fly, he said Taggart's got twenty-five men and at least three crew-served weapons. He said to check and see if there was any way you could find him some reinforcements, local, state, or Federal types, anything you can get."

"Oh my God!"

"Fly, if you can't get any support, he plans to engage Taggart soon after daybreak ... with whatever ordnance you sent him."

"That's crazy! He can't take on twenty men with what I sent him. He's going to get himself killed."

"No he won't. Jessica and I are taking a *lot* more firepower. I don't want to do this without reinforcements, but we aren't going to let the three of them do this alone. If he contacts you before we get to Pinedale, you can tell him we're coming, even if it makes him mad."

"Jesus, Vicky, he's going to be pissed."

"I'd rather he be pissed at us than dead, Fly. Now, get on the horn and find somebody, anybody, who can help!" After a moment's hesitation, she realized she had a very important question to ask Fly that she had neglected to ask earlier ... one that told her she needed to calm down and think clearly before she screwed things up royally.

"Do you know what kind of aircraft that bush pilot has?" The original plan called for the pilot to drop a single equipment bag over the DZ (drop zone) Brad would specify. She and Jessica were adding two human bodies and a substantially heavier bag, and Brad was worried about Taggart hearing the aircraft.

"The only guy I could find willing to stay up all night to wait for a phone call had a DeHavilland DHC-3 Otter. It's a bigger plane than I figure we needed, but it's all I could find ... and it's costing Brad a buttload of money, I can tell you!"

"Not a problem, Fly. It's worth it!" The Dehavilland Otter was a single-engined, high-wing, propeller-driven, short takeoff and landing (STOL) aircraft with an operational service ceiling of over eighteen thousand feet. The craft was designed to carry about nine people and had a maximum takeoff weight of six thousand pounds or more, Vicky couldn't remember. She had used an Otter in an Intelligence op years before, and she remembered thinking that it would be ideal for parachute operations.

Fly had a sharp retort ready, but before she could spit it out Vicky had disconnected the call. Very angry, her fingers flew over the keyboard on her laptop. Seconds later, she was on the phone. Her list of contacts with access to the kind of manpower she needed was short, but reaching out to them at 0130 was not going to be easy. There was no answer at the first phone number she dialed.

* * *

"Our ETA at Ralph Wenz Field is 3:10 a.m. ma'am." The copilot smiled nervously. "Uh, I'm sorry, miss, but you'll need to turn off all electronic devices while we are in flight. We've got the most advanced avionics available on board, and they're kind of sensitive." Vicky reached out absently and switched off the satellite phone.

This was his second trip of the day to Wyoming, but this time there were two ladies—knockouts—aboard. He was more than happy to ferry the ladies, but he'd served in the Air Force before he'd gotten this cushy job flying for Duckworth International Petroleum, and he recognized a 'CIWE' (Case, Individual Weapons & Equipment) bag when he saw one ... and the clanks and the smell of gun oil emanating from the very heavy bag as he carried it aboard for them had confirmed his suspicions.

The earlier bag, the one they had ferried to Pinedale and handed over to a grizzled old bush pilot wearing aviator sunglasses and an Indiana Jones hat and jacket over faded denim jeans, had been kept in the passenger compartment. He'd recognized the outline of M-16s, which had made him nervous enough. This one had bulges that gave him to believe there were automatic weapons inside and even more bulges that looked suspiciously like explosive ordnance ... and that scared the shit of him. They had also carried two parachute packs in with them when they boarded.

To make matters worse, the two women, dressed in faded green tight-fitting coveralls that did nothing to hide some *very* desirable feminine curves, looked mad as hell. He didn't wait for a response, he just darted back to the cockpit and closed the door behind him. Then he leaned back in his seat and locked it.

"What the hell, Bob?" The pilot glared at him.

"Glad we don't have to supply in-flight drinks and meals this trip, Bill. Those chicks are *scary.*"

Bill gave his copilot an incredulous look, but he didn't say anything else. Bob was generally a pretty level-headed guy, and it was highly unusual to see him so stirred up ... especially over a couple of women.

* * *

"You've jumped the ram-air chute before, I know that. My question is whether you've jumped a CIWE bag before."

Jessica and Vicky were about the same size, but Jessica had the stronger build. To the best of Vicky's recollection, the Otter's double doors on the port side were more than adequate for a jumper and CIWE bag, but landing with the bag was tricky. It was not uncommon for a novice to find themselves a bit worse for wear after the first time they tried it.

"I know how." Jessica frowned. "I've seen Brad and Ving do it before. It didn't look that hard to me."

"It's harder than it looks, Jess, and this one is really heavy because of those American 180 drums. As you are well aware, when you get closer to the ground, the ambient light diminishes, and it's hard to judge when to release your lowering line. With a ram-air chute, it's even trickier."

"I think I can handle it."

Vicky decided to try the diplomatic approach. Making contact with Brad and the guys was going to be hard enough without having to nursemaid an overconfident Jessica after they hit the ground.

"Brad was having trouble with his sat phone battery, he said it was almost out of power. Let me handle the CIWE bag, and you focus on trying to locate Taggart's camp. Fly's images showed the glow of their campfires even late at night." Jessica's rebellious expression spurred Vicky to continue.

She opened the topographical map Fly had prepared for them, laminated on both sides with clear acetate, and laid it in Jessica's lap.

"Here"—she pointed with her index finger—"are the coordinates Brad gave me for the DZ. It's fairly level and it appears to be a meadow of some kind, but I can't be sure. There is a lot of scree on the mountain slopes, but that's usually on a steeper grade."

Jessica was slightly exasperated with Vicky's explanation. She was an experienced climber, and she knew a thing or two about mountains ... and topographical maps. In spite of her irritation, she listened carefully as Vicky continued.

"This is Brad's last reported position." She pointed to another tiny grease pencil mark on the map. "I don't think he intends to stay there, I think he's planning on moving to the DZ just before daybreak to collect the bag Fly sent. The problem is that we are going to arrive an hour or two earlier than he expects, and we're either going to have to wait for him or go and find him."

Jessica's eyes widened. She understood the implications perfectly. Running up unexpected on Brad, Ving, or Jared in what was unquestionably hostile environment, and in the dark to boot, could get somebody seriously hurt ... or worse.

"What are you thinking?

"I'm thinking I'll try to contact him by sat phone before we jump. If his phone's not dead, we'll be fine. If we can't communicate, we're going to have to play it by ear. There are too many variables to make a decision right now."

Jessica thought about that for a few seconds. "So you plan on jumping the bag, and you want me to keep my eyes peeled for Brad's and Taggart's camp." "Bingo!" Vicky allowed herself a small smile. Jessica was headstrong at the best of times, and when she was amped up, as they both were at the moment, her willfulness could be problematic. She had made night jumps into hairy situations before. She did *not* know if Jessica had ever made a night jump, and she wasn't going to ask now. They were already committed.

CHAPTER TWELVE

Day Three, 0100 hours

Taggart was fitful and unable to sleep. The incident between Acres, Coates, and the hunters was nagging at him, and Ainsley's cool, assured responses had infuriated him to the point where he'd lost his cool in front of his men. Being able to lead these men, most of them anyway, was the core of his ambitions, his plan for the future. Leading them now, in the wilderness, with damn few creature comforts, no women, and only promises of money to come was tenuous enough as it was.

Arming them, feeding them, and paying them a weekly pittance had taken almost all the money from the armored car heist. He could ill afford to show weakness in front of them … and he'd let that rich pansy piss him off to the point where he'd lost it and kicked him in the face. Not cool.

The issue that was plaguing him most at the moment was not, however, the thought of losing the respect of his men. It was the niggling suspicion that something was off kilter about those three hunters.

Jeffries had been adamant that the encounter was mere coincidence, but Taggart didn't believe in coincidence, he was a suspicious man by nature. He had no idea when hunting season was in the Wind River Range, but he'd not seen any hunters since he'd first stumbled on the ruins of this ancient village and decided that it would be the perfect place to hide from the Feds that he *knew* were looking for him. The proprietor at the outpost store had been chock full of information, especially about the high reaches. The guy didn't have much to do, there hadn't been many people around. In the course of their conversation, Taggart had gotten the impression that the area was in kind of an off season.

He had also listened to an interesting conversation among a few old-timers sitting around a genuine antique wooden cracker barrel at the outpost. The conversation centered around an archaeological survey team from Casper College and their discovery of some prehistoric ruins just below the snowline. The team had been excited and talkative when they'd returned to the outpost on the way back from their expedition, but they had not disclosed the location of the site.

"Them fellers wouldn't say one durned thing about where them ruins was," one bearded old man wearing a red flannel shirt, purple suspenders, and faded Levis said.

Another man sitting across the barrel from the first one cackled and slapped his knee. "Din't haveta! If they'd a asked me I coulda told 'em it was up there. My daddy showed me that place when I wuz jist a sprout, taggin' along on one a his elk huntin' trips."

Another toothless old man snorted and then spat into a brass spittoon on the rough wooden floor. "Yore daddy never shot a elk in his life, Eli! Ever'body in the mountains knowed yore daddy lit out once in a while so he could git likkered up an' yore momma wouldn' know about it."

The comment was met with general laughter from all the men circled around the old oaken barrel, but Taggart had been focused on the man with the purple suspenders. He'd waited around until he could catch the old man alone and had engaged him in a long-winded conversation. Eli loved to talk, and Taggart had eventually steered the conversation back to the ruins.

"That survey team, did they leave anybody behind to guard the place?"

Eli looked at him in surprise. "Naw! Why would they? 'Taint nuthin' but some stacked up rocks an' flat places way up the mountain above one a the feeder lakes off Pole Creek. Been up there fer thousands a year 'cordin' to them young fellers. Shoot, them boys won't even be back till next year when the school lets out fer summer vacation."

He shook his head at the foolishness of the college boys. "Nothin' but stacks a rocks ... an most a them has tumbled down over time. I never give it much thought, but come ta think of it, they *was* set up in a kinda half circle jist at the foot of a bluff. Woulda been a safe place ta live I reckon, if 'twerent so dadblamed cold up there alla time. Even with his belly fulla likker my daddy, he wouldn' stay up there overnight. We din't even go that way but once or twice, an' I think he mighta taken a tetch too much from his jug at the time or we wouldn'a gone that way atall."

Taggart had a hell of a time locating the ruins from the old man's description, but he'd had seven men to help him look, and they'd spread out to search. They found the site surprisingly fast, but not once had any of them reported seeing a solitary soul.

Scott Conrad

* * *

"Jeffries!"

Taggart's voice had an ominous note in it, and Jeffries, half dozing by the fire, practically leaped to his feet. He was acting as sergeant of the guard, responsible for making sure the guys in the LP/OP were relieved and keeping the fire burning. It was a shit detail, but Jeffries never complained where the others might hear him. Being the number two honcho to the gunny fed his ego even if Taggart really *was* crazy.

"On the way, Gunny!" He was there in an instant. Taggart was standing in front of his GP Small in a tee shirt and camouflage trousers, in his stocking feet. He was bleary-eyed and he was pissed.

"Roust four of the guys ... not Coates or Acres, them two ain't reliable, I need four of the best. Send 'em out on patrol, Jeffries. I wanna know where them damned hunters went an' what they were doin' out here in the middle a nowhere an' I wanna know right now!"

"But Gunny, it's the middle of the night..."

"No buts, Jeffries. Do what I said an' do it now or I'll find somebody who will."

Jeffries' mouth snapped shut. Taggart was in a dangerous mood and there was only one thing to be said that would calm him down. "Aye aye, Gunny." Jeffries fled to the nearest of the GP Mediums to get four warm bodies.

* * *

"What kind of shit is this? How we gonna track 'em in the dark, Jeffries?" Bannon was shrugging on his camouflage blouse and buttoning it up, irritated at being awakened in the middle of the night.

"Yeah, Jeffries, what the hell?" Foster, another one of the Marine prisoners who had escaped from the prisoner transport detail with Taggart, grumbled as he tied his bootlaces.

The other two ex-Marines were giving Jeffries baleful looks even as they dressed themselves.

"C'mon guys, it's nothing you haven't done before, you did it in the Sandbox and you can do it here."

"People were tryin' ta kill us in the Sandbox, Jeffries, we was at war. Them three guys was just hunters and Acres scared the hell out of 'em. They gotta be miles away from here by now." Bannon snatched up his M-16 angrily.

"You can thank Acres for this then. He wasn't supposed to shoot at them, he was supposed to notify the gunny, not engage them. Gunny's worried, he ordered me to form a patrol and send it out and you're it. That's all you need to know."

"We ain't in the Corps no more," Foster muttered, standing up slowly and cradling his M-16 in his arms like a deer hunter.

Ignoring the comments, Jeffries issued the instructions he'd formulated during his short walk from Taggart's tent to the first troop tent.

"Form up outside. I'll guide you to the LP/OP and point out where the hunters went after Acres shot at them. The moon is still pretty bright tonight, almost like daylight. When you pick up their trail—"

"*If* we pick up their trail..."

Jeffries ignored the sarcastic crack. "When you pick up their trail, spread out in a traveling vee formation and follow it until you find them. Do *not* engage them, understand?"

"What do you want us to do with them, Jeffries?" This from the sarcastic peckerhead.

He allowed some sarcasm of his own to creep into his voice.

"I want you to do what Acres was *supposed* to do, you chowder head... Get back here and notify me or Taggart that you've located them! Taggart is really ticked off right now, so don't fuck it up!" He turned and led them out of the tent, past the central campfire, and down to the LP/OP, hoping he had not chosen the wrong men. Taggart had recruited mostly hard-core pros that performed their assignments with the same diligence they had in the Corps, but there were definitely some jokers in the deck.

"If you haven't located them by daylight, send one man back and I'll send another couple of patrols out."

That lifted their mood a little. Daybreak was a little over four hours off, and the men believed that this meant the men coming out would be in for a very long day, which should also mean they themselves would be able to come back to camp for some serious rack time.

Jeffries pointed out the spot the hunters had been when Acres had stupidly fired on them. The bright moonlight made visibility almost as clear as it would have been in daylight, and the four men moved out reluctantly in a ragged vee formation. Their training and experience quickly overrode their irritation and they fell into their old habits. They'd once been Marines, but for now they were hunters of men ... serious business.

Jeffries turned and looked at the guard watching Ainsley then glanced up at the top of the bluff behind the camp. *Shit! I'd better do that now or the gunny's gonna wise up in an hour or so and I'll have to get up and post a damned sentry up there. I'm kinda surprised he hasn't said anything already.*

Day Three, 0223 hours

A chill wind whipped over them, making them wish they had brought heavier jackets, but none of them spoke of it. Discomfort wasn't a priority for them, it was no stranger and it kept them alert. They had shared the results of the recon, and they knew the game had changed. This was combat now, sheer and simple. They were outmanned and outgunned, and the only real weapons they had were their patience and their experience.

They had been in hiding about two klicks from Taggart's base camp since they'd completed the recon. Brad's gut told him that the safest course of action for Ainsley was to wait until they got some kind of reinforcements. His backup plan was to wait until the air drop arrived before taking any further action … a plan he had little confidence in because of Taggart's superior firepower and the fact that the camp was clearly a defensive position and Ainsley had an armed guard with instructions to kill him at the slightest provocation.

"I ain't likin' this," Jared muttered just loud enough so that Brad could hear him over the rush of the mountain wind.

"What's up?"

"We've been here for hours and nobody's come lookin'. Kinda hard to reconcile that with what I saw at Taggart's camp."

"I thought we was in deep kimchi when that guy shot at us," Ving mumbled around another piece of beef jerky from the Ziploc bag. It wasn't bacon, but it was all he had.

"I expected pursuit, but I'm thinking Taggart believed we were just hunters."

"If he did, he's getting sloppy. You never woulda been so careless, Brad, an' I sure as hell wouldn't."

The sound of a stone rattling down the scree above their hiding place halted their murmured conversation abruptly. Jared signaled to the others that he had visual contact and gently raised his Sharps, bringing it to bear on a formation of four men, well spread out. They were moving cautiously and silently. The lead man had his eyes fixed on the ground in front of him. They were clearly tracking, but they continued on down the scree slope, slower now since one of their number had clumsily scuffed up a loose stone from the scree underfoot.

Crap! We've got about an hour before they follow our trail back to here. It's a damn good thing we kept going downhill and circled back! We'd have been up the creek if we hadn't. I'm pretty sure we could have taken them, there are only four, but I have no doubt that the sound would alert Taggart and his men. If we're going to be of any help at all to Ainsley, we have to move, and we have to do it fast.

Brad eased to his feet, signaling Ving and Jared that they were moving. They had worked together so long that they didn't need words to communicate much in a tactical situation. They silently nodded their understanding, and they moved off in a direction that would take them toward the bluff at the rear of Taggart's camp. He didn't intend to go that far; he needed a little space and some time to think. The pursuit was on, and, even if was half-hearted, Taggart was narrowing down his options.

About five minutes into their retreat, Brad noticed a grove of the tall, slender fir trees about fifty meters ahead and across a wide, clear stream that would confuse the trackers for a bit if he followed the bed a short way. Even Jared would have taken a bit of time to scout both sides of the creek in a three-hundred-sixty-degree pattern to determine where his quarry had entered and exited the water ... and Jared was the best tracker Brad had ever seen.

He'd expected the water to be cold, but it was worse than cold when he took his first careful step into the rushing water, it was freezing. That it was freezing was bad enough, but the bottom consisted of smooth, rounded stones covered with slippery aquatic moss that made it very difficult to walk upright. The stream was broad, and Brad knew he was taking a calculated risk that he would not be exposed and caught midstream. Extremely worried, he signaled back to Ving and Jared to be cautious and then used his fingers to pantomime slipping on the stones underfoot. While he was doing so, it was he who misstepped.

The current was running swiftly around a stone jutting out of the water, one large enough to disrupt the flow and create an eddy that dragged at his trouser leg. His foot slipped out from under him and he went down, half in the frigid snowmelt and half on the exposed stone. He slammed into the top of the stone and it hurt, and he felt a sharp pain in the still healing muscles from the stab wound he'd gotten when a terrorist had cut him while they were rescuing Duckworth in Borneo.

Ving moved forward to help him up, but even as Brad was gasping for breath he was listening for sounds of the four men who were tracking them. He let Ving help him to his feet and then gritted his teeth and indicated they should keep moving. It seemed to take forever to traverse the rest of the distance to the trees, but Brad had recovered from the pain. He slipped his hand up inside his tee shirt and gingerly traced the scar on his side. No blood, a good sign. Then he ran that same hand along his legs from the top of his boot to above his knee until he reached the cargo pocket, and then his blood froze. The satellite phone!

The casing on the phone was clearly cracked, and Brad felt a sinking feeling in his gut as he pushed the power button to see if it still worked. The indicator light wouldn't come on. Heart racing, he opened the case and watched water drip out of the plastic housing. The inside was soaked, and the battery was useless.

There's no way I can communicate with the bush pilot now, and the air drop is scheduled for daybreak. The heavy winds and the necessity for the pilot to fly high enough not to arouse the curiosity of Taggart and company makes it extremely unlikely that he will be able to spot us from the air unless I can figure out a way to signal him from the ground. No way we're going to get the ordnance Fly sent us now ... and there's no way in hell to find out if she found us some reinforcements. We're screwed!

Ving and Jared were scanning the stream bank, searching for signs of the four men tracking them, and didn't notice Brad's look of dismay.

Well, plan A is shot all to hell! Plan B is going to be damned near impossible without the additional ordnance. What are you going to do now, Jacobs? My rifle carries four rounds in its magazine, Jared's is a single shot, and I've no idea how many Ving's holds, but it doesn't matter ... it's not enough.

He finally said it aloud, though he said it quietly so only Ving and Jared could hear him. "Guys, I think we're screwed."

Ving shot him a look and in one shrewd glance took in the dripping satellite phone and the look on Brad's face. His face showed no emotion as he turned back to his scanning of the terrain on the other side of the stream. "We ain't screwed, Brad. We been in worse fixes than this before."

"Maybe so, but I really doubt that Ainsley has. It's him I'm worried about."

"Shock and awe," Jared said with a quiet chuckle. Shock and awe, the technical term for it being rapid dominance, is a method of attack doctrine on the premise of using overwhelming power and spectacular displays of force to create chaos and destroy the enemy's will to fight.

"What's so funny?"

"You've gotten so used ta being able ta create havoc usin' overwhelming firepower, gadgets, an' explosive ordnance that you musta forgot all your tactics classes at Parris Island," Jared said with an easy smile.

"What?"

"He's talkin' 'bout a P.O.W. snatch, Brad." A prisoner of war snatch was a technique employed over the years using a very small force to conduct a surgical strike, in and out as quickly as possible to retrieve a specific prisoner or prisoners without engaging the enemy any more than humanly possible. The P.O.W. snatch, highly refined during the war in Vietnam, had been employed with considerable success by small forces throughout history.

The three of them had been so focused on capturing—or killing—Taggart that they had relegated the rescue of Nicholas Ainsley to a place of secondary importance. Considering what they did for a living these days, that was a cardinal sin. Ainsley may not have hired them, but his safety and freedom had to be their primary objective. All three of them felt a hot flash of shame.

Brad quickly pulled out his topographical map and began a rough sketch of Taggart's camp by the light of the moon. The ordnance wasn't coming, or if it was, they were nowhere near the coordinates where he had specified for them to be dropped and he could no longer communicate with the pilot anyway. That sucked, but there was nothing that could be done about it now. They would have to go with what they had.

Jared smiled. "You gonna let me take out Taggart with the first shot? Cut off the head of the snake?"

Brad didn't look up from his sketching. "Your first shot will have to take out the guard that has orders to shoot Ainsley. *Then* you can take out Taggart."

He lifted the grease pencil from the acetate and studied his handiwork. He frowned and passed the map to Jared. "Add any details you noticed that I left out, and then see if Ving can add to what we've got."

He had done an excellent job of recreating Taggart's camp, so even Jared's excellent eye for detail found little to add to the details Brad had sketched. Ving added only one small detail and an observation.

"Most a them guys was already racked out in them tents, but there were a few settin' around them fires drinkin' beer, like they was just comin' off guard mount ... and that was kinda weird to me because I didn't see any sentries other than the ones posted in the LP/OP."

"You think they've got sentry positions we didn't find?" They were experienced Marines, and they knew each other well enough to know that the recon had been as thorough and detailed as was humanly possible. There was no way there could be a lookout post or sentry position around that camp that they had missed, all of them would have sworn to it. Still...

"It doesn't matter anyway," Jared pointed out. "We're not makin' a frontal assault, just a raid, in an' out before they know what hit 'em."

"You will get their attention for a while until they figure out what's happening," Brad said, tapping a spot on the bluff above the camp. "A covered and concealed position up here is the key to us pulling this off. Ving and I will take care of getting Ainsley out."

"I can't believe there is no sentry up there. No way in hell I'd set up a camp like that without posting a guard up there."

"We need to quit jabberin' and get movin' before that patrol tracks us down."

"I think that stream crossing will keep them busy for a while yet, but you're right, Ving, we need to get moving." He glanced over at Jared. "I never saw a sign of anyone having been posted on top of that bluff. But Taggart wasn't expecting any hostile action. He's suspicious now, he sent that patrol out…"

"Which means I gotta go sneakin' an' peepin' up there ta make sure there ain't no guard to sound the alarm."

"Exactly."

CHAPTER THIRTEEN

Day Three, 0146 hours.

"Farnsworth, I have eyewitness reports from three highly experienced Recon Marines identifying both Taggart and Nicholas Ainsley. What more proof do you need?"

"I'm sorry, Fly, I really am, but I can't go to my superiors with nothing more than an eyewitness report from three guys on a camping trip, no matter who they are. We have a protocol for dealing with sightings and it has worked for us well in the past. Calm down and let us do our damned job." Supervisory Special Agent Aaron Farnsworth was careful not to slam the headset down onto its cradle, even though he really wanted to.

He owed Fly Highsmith a *lot* of favors, but she was trying to call them in at a time when he was busy as a long-tailed cat in a room full of rocking chairs. The brass had pulled out all stops on this manhunt and the pressure from above was brutal. Nobody was getting any rest tonight, that much he was sure of.

What he couldn't figure out was why. Sure, this Taggart guy had escaped, murdered two guards, and pulled off an armored car heist before disappearing into thin air. Okay, that was horrible, but he had half a dozen other cases that were as bad as, if not worse than, Taggart's ... so why the uproar? What was so important about this *one* jarhead? He did *not need* Fly Highsmith dumping any more of a load on his shoulders than he was already carrying, no matter *how* much he owed her.

* * *

Fly's finger scrubbed angrily across the touchpad on her laptop, moving the cursor to the next name on her list of contacts. She hated the touchpad, but in her haste to change clothes and come back to the comm center yesterday, she had left her wireless keyboard and mouse in her own home. It was a major annoyance to have to use the tiny laptop keyboard and the touchpad, but with Vicky and Jessica gone, the only person she could send to get a replacement was Willona, and she was asleep with the boys.

She loved the Texas countryside, and she absolutely adored Brad's ranch, but it sure was inconvenient not being in Dallas, where some of the stores were open twenty-four hours a day. There were stores in the little one-horse towns that dotted the countryside around here, but none of them were open this late at night. Fly sighed. Maybe Willona would go pick up a wireless keyboard and mouse combo for her after she made breakfast for Ving's sons, Jordan and Nathaniel.

The next few names on her list were useless. Three of them were retired and living out of the country, one of them was working with the Department of State on a joint investigation in Guatemala with D.I.A., and one she knew to be on vacation with his family in Fiji.

The next name she came to was one she had already used, Jim Clancy. She hesitated, her finger on the mouse, ready to click on the "call" icon beside Jim's name. When they had talked yesterday afternoon, he had cut her off quickly, using a meeting he was late for as an excuse and pleading the old chestnut of an "ongoing investigation" for not sharing any more intel with her. That crap was for the press, not for somebody like Fly Highsmith. She punched the icon savagely, her temper rising.

The phone wasn't answered until the third ring, and Clancy sounded exhausted.

"Clancy."

"It's me, Clancy."

"Fly, it's almost two in the morning…"

"Listen, I don't have time to fool around with you, this is deadly serious. Brad Jacobs is up near Pinedale, Wyoming and he and two members of his team are sitting on Taggart and company. No contact yet, but if we can't get him some backup I have no doubt that Brad is going to take some kind of action on his own … and he's going to be walking into a trap. Taggart has managed to gather up twenty-five people."

Clancy was scribbling down everything she was saying, forgetting for the moment that his high-tech desk phone was capable of recording the conversation.

"Slow down, Fly, I'm writing this down."

"Oh hell! Hold on a minute, Jim." She stopped to read something that had just popped up onscreen from her search program. "Crap! They just found

Simon Perry's body, Jim. He's been shot. This is just an initial report..."

"Oh Lord!"

"Damnit Jim, he's going to get himself killed!"

"Fly, in order for me to do anything I need a request from local law enforcement. I can't just horn in on a local murder case."

"Simon Perry was *with* Nicholas Ainsley, Jim."

"I understand, Fly, but you know there is a set of criteria that has to be met before we are permitted to get involved. I agree, this makes an abduction much more likely, but I need more."

"I have images from SecureWatch showing the location."

"Live feed?"

"No, I can't access the right programs. DoJ has changed their passwords and login."

"Come on Fly, if you want me to help Mr. Jacobs you've got to give me something more. Hell, we still don't have an official report that Nicholas Ainsley is a missing person yet."

"What the hell is wrong with you people?" Fly was fuming. "None of you had any trouble taking his word for what he saw in Iraq or Afghanistan! He just called in the intel and those guys bombed the crap out of whatever he warned them about!"

"Jacobs was in Iraq?"

"He was in the Marine Corps, Force Recon, and so were the two men with him right now, the ones *you're* going to get killed if you don't get off your ass and help me! For God's sake, Jim, he's found the guys you're looking for and you're not listening to a word I'm saying." She was near tears, but they were tears of frustration and anger. She heard him sigh.

"Don't take this as a promise, Fly, I doubt if I can pull it off, but I'm going to try."

"What?"

"I know a guy, okay? Let's leave it at that for now. You have a way I can get in contact with Mr. Jacobs?"

"I have his satellite phone number, but every time I try to call it all I get is a message saying the phone is not in service or out of range."

Another heavy sigh. "You have his coordinates?"

She gave them to him, first Taggart's camp and then Brad's last known location ... where he had requested the air drop. She considered telling Clancy about Vicky and Jessica and the air insertion, but something told her it was best not to mention that yet. He would probably tell her to get Brad to back off and let the F.B.I. handle it, and she knew the man well enough to know that he would never back off. It just wasn't in him.

"Let me see what I can do, Fly. Can you send me those images you were telling me about?"

Her fingers were already flying as she loaded the images onto his email. He would get better resolution in an email and the exif data would be easier to read and the images could be verified.

"Listen Fly, let me see what I can do, and I'll get back to you, okay?"

"Jim, I can't tell you how I know this, but something's going to happen about daylight, and I'm afraid if we don't get help to him by then it's going to be harsh ... and you wouldn't want anybody to know I told you about this yesterday." There was a sharp, rapid intake of breath on the other end of the call, and then the sound of the call being disconnected. Fly pushed enter and the email was on its way.

Scott Conrad

* * *

Jim Clancy ended the call by slamming the receiver down in its cradle. He owed Fly Highsmith more than he could ever repay her. She'd made a joke about the candy cigarettes, but she hadn't mentioned taking down the man they were supposed to be surveilling at the time. The suspect had somehow discovered that he was being surveilled, and he had followed Clancy to the candy store where he'd gone to satisfy his stupid craving. Fly had intuited that something was wrong and had ended up tailing the suspect as he dogged Clancy.

When Clancy left with the damned candy cigarettes to go back to the motel, the suspect had stepped out of an alleyway and slipped a garrote over his head. If Fly hadn't been there, Clancy would have been found dead in the alleyway where the suspect had dragged him. He reached up and fingered the thin white scar across his throat that he had to cover with his wife's makeup because it wouldn't tan. It was a constant reminder that he owed Fly Highsmith his life.

He set down the pen in his hand and dialed the number she had given him for Jacobs.

"We're sorry. The person at the number you have called is unavailable at this time. Please check the number or try your call again later."

"Damnit!" He slammed the phone down so hard that a tiny crack appeared in the hard plastic. Leaning forward, resting his elbows on the desk, and putting his face in his hands, Clancy searched his brain for a solution. Who would have an armed team capable of taking on twenty-five men with crew-served weapons ... and capable of reaching the Wind River Range before daylight?

There was only one possible answer, and he hated making the call. It would be way outside the normal chain of command, and as far as he knew

Raines was still wrapping up that op in Salt Lake City. He took a deep breath and said a small prayer then dialed Larry Raines' number. He and Larry went way back, back even to their days together at Tulane before either of them had even considered applying for the F.B.I. Raines answered the call on the first ring.

"Raines."

"Clancy here, Larry."

"Hey buddy, how they hanging?"

"Don't sound so happy to hear me, Larry, I'm calling for some help ... major league help."

Raines' voice changed timbre, he sounded cautious. "What's up?"

"You familiar with the name Nicholas Ainsley?"

"Multi-billionaire techno geek, always seen with a gorgeous babe or two hanging on his arm?"

"That's the one."

"Yeah, what about him?"

Clancy took a deep breath. "I have a solid report that he's been spotted in the Wind River Region and that he's been captured by a real badass that we're looking all over the country for." He could hear Raines' keyboard clicking in the silence.

"There's no missing persons report on Ainsley... Jim, just how solid is this sighting?"

"I knew there was no missing persons report, but this is solid gold. Got it from Fly Highsmith."

"How the hell does she know about it? Last I heard she was retired and living on a horse ranch near Dallas."

"Well, she's in Dallas, but she's working for a guy, retired Force Recon, headquartered out of some hick town northwest of Dallas."

"Team Dallas?"

"You've heard of them?"

"Yeah, they do the same thing we do. The director has fits every time they pull a mission off successfully, and they've never failed to my knowledge." There was silence on the other end of the phone for a long few seconds. "I'll be damned! Fly got this straight from Brad Jacobs?"

"You know him?" Clancy was surprised.

"Hell yes I know him. Met him at my wedding, he served under my father-in-law in Iraq." Sandy Raines' maiden name was Lingenfelter. "To hear the colonel talk about him, this guy Jacobs is a regular legend in his own time. He sure as hell has the credentials to back that up."

"Yeah, well, he's in deep shit right now. Jacobs and two other members of his team are up there on a camping trip, and they stumbled onto Harlan

Taggart and about twenty or so other guys up there. If I can't get them some backup pronto, there's going to be a bloodbath up there. All Jacobs and his guys have with them is a couple of hunting rifles. Taggart's bunch has crew-served weapons."

"Jesus! Can't he get his team together? I've seen the after action reports on his missions, the ones prepared by D.I.A. and N.S.A., and going against the odds seems to be his thing."

"Larry, this is an urgent request from Fly Highsmith, through me. We wouldn't be asking if there was any other way ... and there's one more thing. Simon Perry, Ainsley's number two? A game warden found his body late yesterday afternoon. His name is being withheld from the public pending notification of next of kin. He was up there camping with Ainsley." Clancy heard his friend sigh.

"I'm in the air, on my way back to Quantico after a rescue mission in Salt Lake City. We are due to start stand down (time when F.B.I. personnel on twenty-four-hour call can take personal leave)." Another pause. "I can't believe I'm doing this, Jim, but I'm going to find out if the local airport can handle this plane and then divert to it, or the closest one that can. I need you to do a couple of things. First, get hold of Ainsley's security team and find out why there's been no MP Report made. Next, email me everything you've got on Jacobs' exact location."

"Got it!"

"Jesus, Larry, if this doesn't pan out the director's going to have my ass..."

"Yeah," Clancy agreed, "but if it does you could end up with a decoration and a fat promotion." He was already forwarding the emails Fly had sent him such a short time ago. "Besides, wouldn't it be a feather in the director's cap if it got out that you had to come in and rescue Team Dallas?" There was a long silence after that, and Clancy knew he had Raines hooked through the bag.

"Yeah... Well, I got one more thing I need you to do, Jim."

"What's that?"

"Figure out how we're going to get from Ralph Wenz Airport to these coordinates you sent me with twenty-two men and their equipment. I can get there in ... a shade under two hours. We're not set up for an airborne operation, Jim."

"I'm on it, Larry, as soon as we're off this call. I'll keep you abreast of developments as they unfold."

"Keep your fingers crossed, Jim. If the shit hits the fan over this you and Sandy may have to put Becky, me, and the kids up till I can get another job."

"I will, Larry, but I'm right there with you."

* * *

The first order of business was a call to Nolan Shepard out in California. It took a bit of verbal intimidation to do it, but he was finally put through to Ainsley's security chief.

Shepard was angry at being awakened. "Shepard," he growled. The only people who had the number to his "red" cell phone were the comm center night operator, Nick Ainsley, and Simon Perry. It was rare for him to receive a call after hours from anyone other than the night operator. He could hold a pen in one hand and still have enough fingers left to count the times Nick or Simon had called him after hours.

"Nolan Shepard?"

"Who is this? How'd you get this number?" He didn't recognize the voice and he was about to hang up on what he thought was a misdial when he heard Clancy give his name and rank. It changed the tone of the conversation instantly.

"What can I do for the F.B.I. this morning?" He had to bite his tongue to keep from adding "sir" to the end of the sentence.

"Why haven't you filed a missing person's report on Nicholas Ainsley yet?"

"There must be some mistake. Nick isn't missing; he's fishing up in Wyoming with his number two man, Simon Perry, and his assistant…"

Clancy fell silent for just a few seconds. "You haven't been informed?"

"Informed of what?"

"Do you have the name of Mr. Perry's next of kin?"

"Simon doesn't have any… Oh my God!"

"I didn't tell you anything at all, Mr. Shepard," Clancy said carefully. "You need to remember that."

"Jesus! Do you think Nick—?"

"Has he made contact with you recently?" Clancy interrupted.

Shepard was in panic mode. "No, but that's not unusual... I *told* him it was stupid to go off like that without a security detail!"

If you were any kind of professional you would have gone with him yourself. He didn't say it out loud though, Shepard was genuinely disturbed. It didn't change his opinion one bit.

"Mr. Shepard, I don't know your security protocols, but I highly suggest you contact the proper authorities immediately."

"But you're the F.B.I."

"And we can't get directly involved unless we are requested to do so by the local authorities, so I suggest that if you have any political pull, you contact your senator or representative and raise as much hell as possible about getting us involved.

Time is wasting, Mr. Shepard." He hung up abruptly. *That should light a fire under his ass.*

The next thing on his agenda was to get hold of Fly. They had to find some way of getting Raines and his Blue Team from Ralph Wenz Field out to Jacobs and Taggart, and they had to do it in one hell of a hurry. He dialed her number.

CHAPTER FOURTEEN

Day Three, 0228 hours

Lawrence Raines was ravaged by mixed emotions. He was way out on a limb with the F.B.I., diverting Blue Team without proper authorization from Quantico, but so far nobody back there had noticed. He was doing it because he knew a lot more about Brad Jacobs and his Team Dallas than he'd let on to Jim Clancy.

HRT is constantly conducting training, polishing their skills and keeping up with changes in tactics, techniques, and technology. In the past few months there had been a sea change in those three things, and Raines was one of the few men who knew that the changes were brought about by Jacobs' startling record of successes.

The instructors at Quantico admired Jacobs, one of them had even worked with the man in

Afghanistan and had nothing but glowing praise for the retired Recon Marine. Despite their approval of their hijacking of Jacobs' methods and means, the brass were not about to endorse a man who was doing their job better than they could. Raines knew they envied the man, probably because he didn't have to kiss anybody's ass and didn't have to deal with a bunch of red tape.

He was pissed off and excited at the same time. On the pissed off side, his men had earned their stand down time and they were crashing from the rush of this last mission. When the adrenaline from a good op left you, it left a man feeling emotionally and physically drained. Added to the psychological crash, Clancy had only forwarded him copies of static satellite images that were at least two days old. At least they had two sets of GPS coordinates to go on.

He logged in to the SecureWatch site and groaned when he learned that no satellite with live action thermal imaging capability would be within range of the site in the next thirteen hours ... by which time, hopefully, this entire fiasco would be over and done with.

Jacobs and his two men were on the ground in the area but were apparently not in communication with anybody, and that presented a serious, almost insurmountable problem for Blue Team. How to make contact with Jacobs and his men without engaging them—or being engaged by them—inadvertently?

On the good side, he was going to get to work with Brad Jacobs, one of the best, if not *the* best, in the world of hostage rescue. A side benefit to that was the knowledge that, while they outwardly hated the man, the brass would be tickled pink to announce that HRT had been called in to save Jacobs' ass. That wasn't precisely true, they were being called in as reinforcements—to assist—but the brass would definitely put their own spin on it.

I can't wait to tell my father-in-law about this! He's going to be pumped when I tell him about my getting to work with Jacobs in what I truly believe is going to be a serious shooting match!

Raines glanced down the row of seats in the C-130J specially outfitted for HRT's use and crooked his finger at his second in command, Don Matthews. When Matthews noticed him, Raines pointed at Bruce Walker, the Intelligence agent for the team, and indicated that both should come forward to the commander's space at the forward end of the compartment. Raines' in-air office held a desk, a sofa of sorts, a couple of high-tech laptops, and assorted office equipment. The Federal Bureau of Investigation, as did any other government agency, fed on a vast mountain of paperwork.

When the two men, stretching and yawning, reached his little office, he indicated they should close the (relatively) soundproof curtain separating it from the rest of the team and take a seat on the sofa. Walker closed the curtains while Matthews gave Raines a quizzical look.

"I'm going to come right out and say it, guys. As of now we are mission go." Both men sat up bolt upright on the sofa. "The next thing I have to say is that this is a command decision for which I assume full responsibility." Matthews' bushy right eyebrow crawled up into a question mark, but Walker's face remained impassive.

Raines handed a sheaf of photocopies to Matthews. "I don't know if you're aware of this case, but the Denver Field Office has this guy at the top of their 'Wanted' list. It's a hot potato and they have every available agent on it."

Matthews looked down at a black-and-white photo of Harlan Taggart and then back at Raines. "And this involves us how?" Raines pointed at the sheets and said nothing. Matthews glanced back down at the other papers and read a bit about Taggart. "Larry, come on, let the other shoe drop. We don't normally get involved with an escaped prisoner, even if he is a murderer and a robber."

"Not a bank, Don," Walker commented, taking one of the sheets from Matthews. "An armored car … and according to this, he's killed at least four people since he escaped."

"It may be five," Raines said. "Late yesterday afternoon, the body of Simon Perry, close friend and associate of Nicholas Ainsley, was found shot to death just a mile or two from a remote outpost store near Pinedale, Wyoming."

"What ties that to Taggart?"

"Bruce, we have what I would call a reliable source that reports seeing Nicholas Ainsley being chased through the mountains by Taggart and several men, not too far from where Perry's body was found. Ainsley and Perry were in this area fishing."

"But…"

Raines ignored Matthews' protest. "To complicate matters even further, just a few minutes ago, I got a personal call from Senator Perkins of the Committee on the Judiciary, the oversight committee that keeps an eye on law enforcement agencies, and he is extremely anxious that we go ahead and start this mission without waiting for the Bureau to sign off on it. He is, at this moment, I believe, chewing on the director's ear on Mr. Ainsley's behalf."

Walker laughed. "I'd love to listen in on *that* conversation." The Director was not a fan of politicians who thought they knew better than he how to run the Bureau, even ones on the Senate Committee on the Judiciary.

"So you're expecting a call from the director at any minute..."

"So who's your reliable source and how do we know it was really Taggart they saw?" Matthews, as second in command, saw it as his job to play devil's advocate, and Raines agreed with him. In front of the men, Matthews never questioned Rains or his decisions, but in private he always helped by picking apart the smallest details and forcing Raines to evaluate each of them. They worked well together.

"Out of school?"

"Hell, Larry, this whole thing is out of school…"

"You've heard of him. It's Brad Jacobs."

"Team Dallas Brad Jacobs? That Brad Jacobs?"

Raines nodded. Matthews chewed on that for a moment and then he got a skeptical look on his face. "Okay, I've heard of him all right, and I'm impressed, the guy knows what he's doing. My question is how do we know he's certain that it was Taggart chasing Ainsley? Ainsley is a public figure, and I expect anyone who's read a magazine, a newspaper, or watched television in the last five years would recognize him, but Taggart is a nobody."

Raines smiled and tapped the sheaf of papers in Matthews' hand. "Because he knows him personally. Moreover, the two men with Jacobs know him too. The four of them were all with the Marine Corps at the Second Battle of Fallujah."

Walker let out a low whistle.

"I'd say that's pretty reliable. Way better than most eyewitness sightings we get," Matthews, chagrined, had to agree.

"So where the hell is this place we're going?"

"The Wind River Range, about fifteen miles northeast of Pinedale, Wyoming." He punched a key on his laptop and a map materialized on the monitor. "I have 1:25,000 topographical maps over there by the printer, but I can project this one onto the big screen over there. The terrain is a real bitch."

Matthews and Walker craned their necks to look at the forty-eight-inch color television and Raines punched another key on his laptop. The map opened on the screen in glorious color.

"Gentlemen, I believe we have some work to do."

"I just hope the Bureau doesn't hand us our asses for this," Matthews groused.

"When you finish reading those copies, I think you'll find there is more to worry about than the Bureau."

* * *

"Wow! This Taggart guy is a real sonofabitch." Walker shuffled a few papers and found the one he wanted. "It says here he was suspected of committing atrocities against civilians in Iraq. The convening authority decided they didn't have enough evidence to convict, so he was given non-judicial punishment. Up until last year this guy had some kind of guardian angel looking over him, but they finally got him last August at Pendleton."

"What for, Bruce?" Matthews looked up from the satellite images he was perusing.

"Says he got into it with an officer and beat the hell out of him. After the court martial he was sentenced to ten years at Leavenworth."

"Sounds like his guardian angel took a hike."

"Yeah, in spades. He and seven other prisoners managed to escape during a flight transfer. The two guards assigned to the prisoner detail were brutally murdered at the Denver airport, their bodies stuffed into a trash chute in one of the men's rooms. Took the supervisor twenty or so minutes to decide to go check on them, and by then Taggart and the others were already gone."

"Damn!"

"It gets better. Somehow they managed to get civilian clothes and stage an armored car heist in front of a bank in broad daylight. They killed the driver and the courier, stole their weapons, and made off with a buttload of cash ... technically not a bank robbery because it took place in the street outside before the courier ever went inside."

"No witnesses?"

"None that could give more than a rudimentary description of the perps, but we got lucky and a security cam across the street from the bank enabled an analyst to identify Taggart after a little enhancement."

Raines sighed. "That'll be suppressed in court because of the enhancement if he gets even a half-assed lawyer."

"The Denver Field Office put out a bolo after they wasted a couple of days looking for him themselves. After that, they started getting reports of sightings from all over. Local cops get a little hyper when the Bureau puts out a bolo for 'armed and dangerous.' You can't blame them."

"Any of the sightings pan out, Bruce?" Matthews was doggedly determined to play out his role until the mission plan was set.

"Not yet, but you know the selection protocol as well as I do, Don. Each alleged sighting is assessed by admin staff then assigned to and pursued by the closest agents available. It's an enormous drain on personnel resources and it's time consuming."

"Yeah," said Raines, "and according to Highsmith, time is the one thing Ainsley doesn't have enough of. We already know his associate was murdered, and according to her, Jacobs' assessment is that Taggart's going to kill him sooner or later, ransom or not."

"Has anyone contacted Ainsley's company about ransom yet?"

Raines shook his head, a thoughtful look on his face. "Not unless Shepard was lying to me ... and if he was, he did a damned fine job of it. He wasn't even aware that Perry had been found dead yet, and he didn't file his missing persons report on Ainsley until after I called him. Told me it wasn't unusual for Ainsley to be out of contact for a few days when he goes off to take a break and let off a little steam. Doesn't happen very often."

Matthews changed the subject. "Any word from Fly on transport to the sight from the airport yet?" The aviation assets that usually accompanied the team on missions had been sent to their aviation support facility at HRT Central Command for maintenance, refit, and upgrades because of the scheduled two-week stand-down.

"Not yet." Raines stretched in his chair, his arms akimbo and his fists clenching as he yawned. When he was through, he glanced at the Breitling diver's watch on his wrist. "I need to call her, we've got less than an hour before we touch down. Don, why don't you give a heads up to the team while I make the call? Bruce, when I'm done with her, I want to go over the site evaluation and the movement plan."

"Sure thing, Larry, I'll be able to finalize the movement plan as soon as you get me the mode of transport." He was inwardly glad this wasn't an airborne operation. He could do it if he had to, but it scared the hell out of him every time they had a practice jump on a training exercise. The team had never had a real-world mission that required airborne insertion. The worst they'd had so far was the fast-rope insertion, and that was bad enough.

* * *

"Fly? Larry."

"I was just about to call you. You aren't going to believe this, but I've laid on a CH-47 for you. Guy charters it for remote high-altitude construction projects in the mountains. His business has a Triple A rating and a perfect flight safety record."

"A Chinook in *Pinedale*?" The CH-47 Chinook, manufactured by Boeing, is a twin-engined, tandem rotor, heavy-lift helicopter capable of carrying a payload of 24,000 pounds. The CH-47 is among the heaviest lifting Western helicopters. It is used extensively by the U.S. military and by many other countries as a transport helicopter.

"I was as surprised as you are, but there is one there in great shape and the owner is running it up right this minute so that you can board it the minute your plane stops rolling."

"I'm impressed, Fly!"

"You should be. It just cost me a helluva pile of money to set this up."

"If we end up getting approval, Fly, I'll see to it you're reimbursed. If not, I'm going to come looking for a job."

"I hear you, Larry. Good luck!" Fly was going to mention that Vicky and Jessica were en route to Pinedale as well (though she was a little worried because she hadn't heard from them for a while), but Raines had already hung up.

CHAPTER FIFTEEN

Day Three, 0319 hours

They rushed down the steps of the Gulfstream and waited anxiously for the copilot to open the luggage compartment. Vicky scanned the small airport until she located the DeHavilland Otter.

"There's our aircraft." The plane was sitting on retractable wheels surrounded by pontoons for water landings. There were apparently no airport personnel on duty, but Vicky spotted a baggage cart over near the terminal building. "Would you get that, Jess?" She pointed at the cart. It was going to be bad enough having to lug the CIWE bag around the mountains for however long it took to meet up with Brad without having to lug it, their rucksacks, and the parachutes around the airport. The parachutes weren't a problem once they got on the ground, they could stash them and recover them later.

Jessica ran to the terminal and then ran back, pushing the baggage cart in front of her. The aluminum cart made a loud rattling sound as it rolled across the tarmac.

"We'll get those," Vicky told the copilot, who was just as happy to let the red-haired Amazon and her blonde companion handle the menacing bags and the parachutes. They were pretty as hell, but he didn't think he'd want to tangle with either of them. They looked like avenging angels to him. They had the cart loaded and in motion even before the copilot had started his preflight inspection.

"I don't see our bush pilot," Jessica said, glancing over at the Otter.

"He didn't know for sure what time we'd get here. He's probably in the pilots' lounge catching a nap. We'll probably have to go wake him up."

That didn't prove necessary. A lot of money had changed hands because of the inconvenient hour, and even more had changed hands to ensure the bush pilot at Ralph Wenz Field would have his aircraft warmed up and ready for takeoff the minute Vicky and Jess could offload the jet. The pilot, an older, bearded man wearing a flight jacket, jeans, boots, and a ball cap came strolling out from behind the Otter, wiping his hands with a dirty red rag.

"Sorry ladies, had to help my buddy get his bird ready. This has been one weird day. First you two and this 'urgent' charter, and then Calvin gets a call for an 'urgent' charter in the middle of the night." He grinned. "I don't usually fly at night anymore, but the money was too good to pass up. I can't even imagine what Calvin's getting to fire up that beast of his this early in the morning, but it must be a hell of a lot for him to crawl out of his warm bed and come out here at this time. He won't be here for a bit, his place is the other side of Pinedale.

"I'm Sam Tullis, by the way," he said, extending his hand. Vicky shook it briefly but didn't bother to introduce herself, and then she turned to beckon for Jessica to bring the cart as she began to walk over toward the Otter.

"I already did the preflight and ran the motor up before you landed," Tullis said as he tried to match Vicky's long-legged stride. It was kind of comical because he was a good six inches shorter than she was.

He looked back at Jessica for a moment and noticed the two parachute packs. "You aren't planning on jumping tonight, are you?" He gave the two women a once over and did a double take. He hadn't paid any attention to the way they were dressed until then. Vicky didn't answer.

"The cargo door? We're really in a hurry, Sam." She gave him a seductive smile that made him feel like a horny teenager inside and he hurried to open the double doors on the port side of the Otter.

Despite the weight of the CIWE bag, the two women loaded their gear into the cargo bay quickly. Vicky climbed aboard while Jessica returned the baggage cart to the terminal at a dead run.

"Get this thing started, Sam."

The old pilot didn't understand why they were in such an all-fired hurry, but he shrugged it off. He'd been wanting to buy a new snowmobile for the last couple of years, and this one charter was going to pay for a beaut. He opened the door to the cockpit and climbed in. Jessica reached the aircraft just as the turboprop engine began to whine and the propeller started to rotate.

After what seemed to Vicky to be an interminable wait, the Otter began to creep forward.

"Wow! I didn't even know civilians could own one of those!"

Vicki turned to look out the starboard window and noticed an older but well-kept white-over-red CH-47 Chinook.

"Yep," Sam called out over the growing whine of the turboprop. "That's Calvin's bird. It has a hell of a service ceiling, and he gets a lot of construction projects in the mountains around here. Rich folks don't seem to mind building those whatchamacallits, chalets, up here in the middle of nowhere ... and, of course, there are several resorts scattered around and they're always needing something heavy moved in or adding new buildings. Calvin's the only one around with that kind of capability."

The whine of the turboprop got louder, and Sam shoved a couple of headsets at Vicky and pointed at his ears. Then he turned and advanced the throttles until the plane was shaking and then released the brakes. They were rolling. In almost no time he pulled back the wheel and the Otter rotated upward at a steep angle.

Vicky slipped on her headset and handed the other to Jessica. Then she turned and slid to the front of the cargo compartment to watch the altimeter on the control panel.

"You flying VFR (Visual Flight Rules)?"

Sam chuckled into the headset. "Sure am, lady. There ain't much traffic up here under thirty thousand feet, and this baby"—he patted the dashboard—"don't go that high. I only fly IFR (Instrument Flight Rules) when the weather gets rotten."

"I need you to climb to reach and hold an altitude of about twelve thousand feet. Can you do that for me, Sam?"

Sam turned his head to stare at the red-haired siren as if she was insane. "Lady, you ain't thinking of jumping out of this plane tonight, are you? I was told I had to make an air drop when I first took the charter, but when I heard you two were coming, I naturally thought we were going to make a water landing on the lake."

"We're still making an air drop, Sam, only it will be us and our equipment instead of just a bag."

"At twelve thousand feet the winds are going to be awful, and it's going to be freezing cold. If you don't already know this, that ground down there is rocky and just plain dangerous for somebody who's unfamiliar with it."

"We've done it before, Sam. I spent a lot of years in the military, and as you boys say up here in the mountains, 'this ain't my first rodeo.'" She batted her eyes outrageously and gave him her sexiest smile. "Jessica and I are experienced jumpers."

Tullis' mouth snapped shut and he turned again to his instrument panel. It was no skin off his nose if this woman and her friend wanted to skydive in the middle of the night and maybe get themselves killed. He just wished they hadn't chosen his plane to do it from. Still, there was the money. He hadn't asked when that Highsmith woman had mentioned the sum, and it was his own fault for agreeing to the charter without asking any questions. It really *was* a lot of money.

* * *

The ride had gotten a little bumpy, and it was difficult to strap on the parachute harnesses, but they managed. Hooking their rucksacks to the front, beneath the small reserve chutes, was harder, but when it came to attaching the CIWE Vicky needed Jessica's help.

Jessica switched off her headset. "I'm going to take my weapons out of this bag and put them in the smaller case, Vicky. At least I can lighten your load by a little." She opened the CIWE bag and withdrew her rifle and the M-79, as well as a half dozen rounds for it. "Want me to take a couple of the drum magazines as well?"

"No, Brad and Ving—oh my God! Jess, I never turned my sat phone back on! I need to call and see if Brad is answering his yet!" She had wondered why Fly hadn't called them back, and now she knew why. She fumbled in her cargo pocket and pulled out the phone, switching it on. There were three missed calls, all from Fly.

"Open the doors," Tullis called out. We'll be over the drop zone in one minute."

"I can't believe I forgot this!" Vicky uttered some very unladylike words as she speed dialed Brad's number. She got the same message again. There was no time left to place a call to Fly.

"Twenty seconds!"

Vicky slipped on her goggles and staggered over to the doors Jessica had locked open and grabbed the overhead hand rail with one hand. Her other hand held the drogue chute that would open her main. Tullis had been right, the air was so frigid that her skin was turning blue and she was shivering.

"Ten seconds!"

Jessica grabbed the overhead bar and her own drogue chute. Vicky would exit first, Jessica going second to make sure Vicky or the CIWE didn't get hung up on the aircraft.

"Go!" They jumped out into the moonlit night.

Vicky had always hated those first few seconds of freefall before the drogue chute pulled the canopy and suspension lines out and inflated. At twelve thousand feet there wasn't much darkness, she could see the ground as if it was twilight. Well to her north she could see the faint semicircle of fires of Taggart's camp, just like she had seen it on Fly's computer images ... only they were twinkling now instead of giving off a steady light. The camp appeared to be a very long way off. There was no sign of fires or light anywhere beneath them where Brad was supposed to be waiting. Vicky felt a chill in her chest that had nothing to do with the jump.

The winds tugged fiercely at her face, and she had a hard time keeping the chute steered into it. Jessica, having jumped after her, was floating somewhere above her. Vicky dropped her eyes back to the ground, which was rushing toward her with far more speed than it usually did thanks to the added weight of the CIWE bag. There was no sign of the guys anywhere beneath her feet. She uttered a silent prayer that Brad, Ving, and Jared were okay, but she kept her eyes open. Landing was going to be a bitch. No more time to look for Brad, she had to concentrate on finding the best spot to land.

* * *

Vicky was much lower than she was, and Jessica reached for the risers and dipped the canopy downward and to the left, causing the chute to spiral and increasing the speed of her own descent. She wasn't worried about the rate of descent, all she had to do was make sure she was facing into the wind just before the landing. Then pull both toggles down and flare. The technique was second nature to her. The only thing she was worried about was Vicky. The CIWE bag was heavy as hell, and if Vicky had to struggle with the weight, she wouldn't get to collapse her chute fast enough and she could be dragged by the winds. It had happened to Jessica a couple of times when she first learned to jump. It wasn't fun.

She had seen the light from Taggart's fires, but there had been no sign of Brad, Ving, and Jared. *They must be worried about Taggart spotting them, otherwise there'd be a triangle composed of three lights to mark the DZ. Damn! I smell trouble, and there's no way to determine what it is or which direction it is coming at me from. Brad has preached at me since I was a kid. "Trust your instincts!" So far he's been proven right...*

She halted her downward spiral and faced into the wind then released her lowering line. She didn't have to watch the ground, she felt her rucksack strike and hauled on the risers to begin her flare. In front of her, Vicky hit the ground pretty hard, a gust of wind had made her botch the flare out, and she was down. Jessica made the mistake of trying to alter her landing point, and it cost her. Another gust of wind caught her and tilted the canopy to the right. Her right foot caught on her own rucksack and her ankle twisted sharply. A sharp pain shot through her ankle and flashed up her leg, and then she was on the ground.

Desperately she hauled on the suspension lines billowing around her as the canopy flapped in the wind, trying to collapse it before it could drag her across the ground. She was only partially successful, the chute dragging her painfully across several yards of stony ground before she managed to collapse the canopy.

She struggled to her feet and found that she could stand, even though her ankle hurt like blazes. Vicky was wrestling with her canopy several yards away, so Jessica limped over to help her as best she could.

Together they got Vicky's chute collapsed, and Vicky checked the broad stony meadow they were standing in. She saw no sign of life at all, and the only sound she heard was the rush of the wind. Tullis and his Otter were gone. "We need to get the hell out of this open spot," she whispered. "Can you walk?" She glanced down at Jessica's leg.

"Yeah. It's nothing, just twisted my ankle that's all."

Vicky was concerned, but she didn't say anything. She opened the CIWE bag and removed one of the American 180s instead of the MK-46 she had brought for herself. Jessica got her M-16 out of the individual case she'd jumped, slammed a fully charged magazine into the magazine well, and pulled back the charging handle, letting the bolt slide forward and jacking a round into the chamber. When they were both locked and loaded, they eased their rucksacks on and Vicky shouldered the heavy CIWE bag. Then they walked, Vicky encumbered by the bag and Jessica following, limping badly on her injured ankle. They still hadn't seen hide nor hair of Brad, Ving, or Jared.

"I've got to stop for a minute, Vicky."

Vicky turned to see Jessica sink to the ground and begin fumbling with her bootlaces. "Are you sure you shouldn't sit this out, Jess?" She knew Jessica's answer before she even asked the question but felt obligated to ask anyway. Jessica's ankle was going to slow her down, and considering their situation, that was bad. Even so, she knew she couldn't just leave her behind.

"No way! I just have to tighten these laces up. I can make it." She grimaced and pulled the laces as tight as she could.

Vicky knelt down and reached for her sat phone. She didn't dare call Brad. There was no telling where he was, and the sound of his satellite phone ringing might give away his position and get him killed ... if he even had it turned on. Maybe he had called Fly. She punched Fly's speed dial number. Nothing happened.

Frustrated, Vicky tried to power cycle the device but to no avail. The phone was dead. *How in the hell did that happen?*

Jessica stood and tested her ankle by putting her full weight on it. It still hurt, but it would hold. "I can walk on it." Her voice was full of determination.

"I don't know how far we're going to have to go, Jess. The phone isn't working and I can't contact either Fly or Brad. We're on our own."

CHAPTER SIXTEEN

Day Three 0230 hours.

He made up his mind. "We can't wait for the weapons drop, guys, we're going to have to go with what we've got. I'm worried about Ainsley... I don't trust Taggart not to do something stupid." Ving and Jared nodded grimly.

"If I can get on top of that bluff, I can take out Ainsley's guard with my Sharps, but one of you will need to be as close to Ainsley as you can get because when I drop that guard, all hell is gonna break loose. You'll have to move fast or we're never gonna be able to get out of there. I'm trying to figure out whether to go for the crew-served gunners next or go for Taggart..."

"I'll do the infiltration from the east side. Ving, you take up a position from where you think you can best provide covering fire."

Ving shook his head no and interrupted, something he rarely did. "No way, Brad. I'm doin' the infiltration. You ain't a hundred percent yet an' you know it. That dude in Borneo stuck you good, an' ta tell ya the truth, I was worried for a little while there that you wasn't gonna make it."

"He's right, Brad. He should do the infiltration. You'll be able to increase our chances of success by taking out one of the crew-served gunners when I take out the guard."

Brad scowled. It was infuriating to even admit it to himself, but it was really embarrassing to have to admit it to the two men closest to him. To his credit, he refused to let his feelings override Ving's and Jared's honest evaluation; he knew they were right.

"We have to do this at first light, that's the time when the guys who stayed awake all night on guard are sleepy and the ones who just woke up are still sleep fogged." He was babbling to cover his embarrassment and he knew it. Ving and Jared understood the principle behind a dawn raid as well as he did.

"We move together till we get about a klick from the camp, and then, Jared, you split off and head for that bluff. Ving and I will give you—" he glanced down at his watch "—half an hour then we'll move into position. I want to be set when you initiate the snatch."

"We'd better get movin' then. No tellin' when that patrol will be catchin' up with us."

"Maybe we could ambush 'em and take a coupla them M-16s…"

"No way, Ving. Taggart would hear us if we fired our weapons, and we're in no shape to take on four armed men in a spread vee formation with knives." He didn't have to add that it was his own temporary limitations that he doubted. It was time to discuss the route they would take.

"I think the best approach is going to be to move to the northwest and then curve back around to the bluff ... come in from their blind side. It looks like there's more tree cover that way."

The team had an S.O.P. (Standard Operating Procedure) that covered the minutia generally specified in a patrol Operations Order. The minutia included actions to take or not take for almost any eventuality on a patrol. The Operations Order is structured to organize a patrol into five easily understood paragraphs: Situation, Mission, Execution, Admin & Logistics and Command and Control. In a hasty OpOrder, such as the one they were having now, any changes to the S.O.P. were specifically noted in the briefing. Everything else remained the same per the team S.O.P.

The three men had worked together for so long that their actions on crossing a danger area, actions on hostile contact, and a hundred other details were so ingrained in their minds that everything they did was instantly synchronized. As a result, an OpOrder that would normally take an hour or more to disseminate to a patrol took Team Dallas only fifteen minutes or so.

There was precious little equipment to check. None of them had ammunition of the same caliber so they couldn't share it out, and the only food any of them carried was Ving's jerky. The only thing they had to check, and each of them did so out of long habit, was their water supply. Finally, each of them checked to see if they had anything on their persons that would rattle or clank during movement.

They were ready to move out, and they did so, Jared on point followed by Ving, and Brad bringing up the rear. Five klicks was not a great distance to cover, but the route Brad had specified was a little longer, and they moved slowly and cautiously.

None of them had much faith in the plan, but they had faith in each other ... and all three were firmly convinced that the mission was one they could not turn their backs on. Nicholas Ainsley was in dire straits, and Harlan Taggart was a genuine menace to anyone who crossed his path. The fact that they each had a score to settle with the man factored heavily into their considerations, Jared's perhaps most of all.

Day Three, 0347 hours.

Byron Ashworth awakened to the faint buzz of an aircraft engine far above him. His mouth was parched and he couldn't remember ever having felt so weak and drained. His clothes were wet and smelled sour, and so was the sleeping bag he was lying on. A blinding headache made every movement pure agony, but he was so thirsty that he risked reaching for his canteen.

He fumbled with the cap, finally twisting it off, and then drank thirstily. He swallowed half of the contents before his stomach rebelled and made a supreme effort not to regurgitate the water, but he was only partially successful. He dropped back onto the damp down-filled sleeping bag, too weak to even try to clean up the mess he'd made. *Where are Nick and Simon? Why haven't they come back?* He drifted back into unconsciousness.

* * *

They drifted down from the lake, following the man-smell. Slinking along almost on their bellies, they entered the small half circle of tents, sniffing the air. The stone fire pit reeked of burnt wood, an unpleasant odor that reminded them of the deadly forest fires of summer. The man-shelters were another matter entirely. Two of them bore the tantalizing aroma of man and food, but the third reeked of disease but not death yet. The third one was occupied, but the sickness smell was not one they found pleasing. The leader of the wolf pack sniffed at the tent flap and stared at the recumbent body of the man inside. The sick smell was coming from him. Lifting his hind leg, the leader urinated at the flap opening then wrinkled his nose up and strode away.

The cold season was not here yet, and his belly was not shrunken and painful. In the cold times he would have eaten the sick man and been grateful for the meal, but tonight, ahhh, tonight, there was other prey afoot, warm-blooded, fresh, and tasty. There was no smell of sickness in their spoor. He stole away, blowing the stink out of his nostrils so that he could better follow the spoor of the men who were not sick. Easy prey.

* * *

Nicholas Ainsley awoke with a start. His jaw was swollen where Taggart had kicked him, and it throbbed. His guard was staring up into the sky, bored out of his skull, and another man was tossing a couple of logs onto the fire. Nick watched as the deep, glowing embers caught at the bark on the logs, and tiny tendrils of flame began to lick up the sides. In no time the flames were leaping high, and crackling and popping sounds emanated from the fire pit as pockets of sap exploded along with insects that had been unfortunate enough to select those particular pieces of wood to crawl upon.

His wrists hurt from the tight steel bands of the handcuffs that secured his arms around the rough pole he was leaning against. Stiffness radiated from his neck down into his shoulders and back and ended at the numbness in his hands. His tailbone pressed against the stony ground, and if it hadn't gone numb it would have hurt too. His calf was hot and swollen, and the pain was monstrous.

If you concentrate on the pain you're just going to make it that much worse, Nicky boy. Focus. What can you do to make things better? He shrugged his shoulders, flexing his muscles as much as his restraints would allow. When he shuffled his feet, his injured calf sent a bolt of pain shooting up into his thigh, but he could move his leg. His feet were numb so he clenched and unclenched his toes inside his boots to get the blood circulating. The handcuffs rattled and he looked up to see his guard staring down at him, the M-16 in his hands pointing menacingly in his direction.

Nick managed a crooked grin. "Just stretching a little. It's cold out here you know." The guard said nothing. "You don't suppose I could get a cup of that coffee over there, do you?" The guard glared at him, but he spoke to the man they had called Jeffries, who was squatting down beside the fire sipping coffee from a blue porcelain-coated tin cup. He had just filled the cup from the matching coffee pot resting on three stones of the same size. There was a pile of those glowing coals from the bed of the fire beneath the pot, and steam was rising from the spout. The aroma was strong and tantalizing, even over the smell of the wood smoke.

"Jeffries!" The guard called out. Jeffries looked back over his shoulder without shifting from his squatting position, which made Nick think of that old movie *The Exorcist*, when the little girl's head turned all the way around. Despite his dismal circumstances and the pain wracking his body, he had to stifle a smile.

Jeffries stared at Nick for a moment then made a disgusted grimace. He rose to his feet and dumped his coffee into the fire before going over to a Lister bag suspended from a tripod of thick tree limbs and rinsing the cup out. He poured fresh coffee into the cup and strode over to where Nicholas sprawled against the pole.

"Here," Jeffries said, holding the cup out to Nick. Nick glanced at him mutely, unwilling to mention the fact that he couldn't reach out for the cup with his hands cuffed behind the pine log. He cut his eyes down to his bound arms and Jeffries muttered a curse.

"Uncuff him and sit him back down with his arms and legs around the pole. The guard's face remained impassive as he slung his rifle over his shoulder and knelt behind the pole and inserted the key in the handcuffs, one hole at a time. Nick immediately tried to chafe his wrists, but he was quickly rewarded for his efforts when the guard grabbed him roughly by the shoulders and snatched him back behind the upright pole, slamming his face against the log and jerking his arms around it before slapping the cuffs back on him. Pain exploded in his head and he felt blood coming from his mouth and dripping down his chin. He saw stars.

"No funny business!" The guard's voice was surly and resentful.

Nick spat out a bloody tooth and then gingerly explored his mouth until he found which tooth had been knocked out. He found a hole where his right incisor had been. Jeffries, still holding out the coffee cup, said nothing at all.

Nick grunted and accepted the cup awkwardly in two hands then spat out a mouthful of blood, craned his head to one side, and tentatively touched his lips to the tin cup. It was hot, and he had to blow on it before he sipped. The caffeine rush helped, but only just a little.

"Have you called my security chief yet?" The swelling in his jaw had gotten worse when his tooth was knocked out, and his lips felt thick and rubbery. His voice sounded fuzzy and indistinct even to his own ears, but he really needed to know. The only hope he had of rescue depended on Taggart calling the number he had given him.

Jeffries grunted and took the cup from Nick's hand. "The gunny don't tell me what he's doin' an' I don't ask." He stood up and spun on his heel, tossing the rest of the coffee from the cup as he walked back to squat down at his place by the fire. The truth was he had no idea whether Gunny had made the call or not. The man was obsessive about communications security, and the possession or use of communications devices was absolutely forbidden. Gunny kept the satellite phone hidden away in his tent and no one else was permitted to even touch it. This Ainsley guy was an arrogant pain in the ass. Even in captivity he expected—no, demanded—to know what was going on like he was King Shit. Rich guys were all alike. It was time for him to learn that he wasn't in control of *everything*.

Nick was really worried now. If Taggart didn't call Nolan Shepard's special line, no one would know that he and Simon had run afoul of some really bad dudes and it might be a week or more before anyone came looking for them. He felt a pang of grief as the memory of the death of his longtime friend and colleague formed in his chest and sank into his belly like a knot of ice. It simmered there for a bit as shame at his own cowardice in leaving Simon's body washed over him. Then it expanded into full blown, but impotent, fury. His mind raged, but his body was helpless, which fueled his anger even more. There was nothing he could do now but pray Taggart would call Shepard. Nicholas Ainsley was not a praying man, but he closed his eyes anyway and gave it a shot.

* * *

"Hear anything from the director yet?" Matthews had just returned from the aft compartment, where he'd been giving a pep talk and keeping an eye on the men cleaning their weapons. Under the best of circumstances even the most experienced operators could get a little lax in observing the ironclad rule against having a loaded weapon on board an aircraft, and this was not even close to the best of circumstances. They all had been through an exhausting cycle of anticipation, adrenaline rush, adrenaline crash, and now anticipation again in less than a twenty-four-hour period. The men of Blue Team would bear watching.

"I got a call from the deputy assistant director's executive assistant about three minutes before you returned, Don. He said to continue en route but do not deplane until we receive orders to do so." Both men knew that those orders meant that the mission was now a political football and that a deal was being brokered between Quantico and D.C. Raines seethed at the notion that political games were being played when human lives hung in the balance, but he kept his feelings bottled up inside. Political shenanigans were a fact of life in the Bureau ... in any law enforcement organization really.

Matthews glanced down at the face of his cell phone to check the time. "They'd better get off their asses and make a command decision soon. ETA on our arrival at Ralph Wenz Field is fifteen minutes from now."

"We're not going to wait, Don. I'll take the responsibility."

"Larry, if we don't get approval that'll be political suicide…"

"Maybe so, but I won't have any trouble looking myself in the eye every morning when I'm shaving." Raines gazed at his friend, a steady, unwavering look. "I told, you, I'll take full responsibility."

Matthews shook his head sadly. "We've been together a long time, buddy, and I've never doubted you. I'm not going to start now." He turned his head and called out, "Walker!"

"Yeah Don?" Walker was in the aft compartment with the rest of Blue Team.

"Mission go! E.T.A. fifteen!"

"Mission go!" Walker's voice echoed from behind the partition curtains. Raines could hear the excited shuffling from aft.

Matthews smiled. "Well, Magoo, you've done it now."

Raines smiled thinly at the reference to the old short-statured cartoon character who got into comical situations as a result of his extreme near-sightedness, compounded by his tenacious refusal to admit there was a problem. Magoo always came out on top, no matter what kind of difficulties he faced. Raines would be the first to admit that he owed a great deal of his success with the Bureau to his luck. His supervisors would agree, but they would be quick to point out that his luck was due to his native intelligence, his natural instincts, and to his hard work and dedication.

"Let's go over the loading plan for the Chinook one more time, Don," he said, buckling back down to business. "There's not going to be any time for rehearsals, so we have to make sure everything is fixed in our minds." Matthews nodded. The men weren't fully rested from the mission in Salt Lake

City, they were coming off an adrenaline crash, and they were obviously discouraged about having to miss some of their stand-down time. On the plus side, Blue Team was a selection of the best the Bureau had to offer, highly motivated, highly skilled, dedicated professionals.

"Fly said the chopper was used in construction operations, so I'm going to operate under the assumption that the canvas troop seats are not going to be available. I want the team split in two, one half on each side of the fuselage. You and Bruce will sit on the floor just aft of the cockpit with me. I hope the pilots are as good as she said they were. I'm going to direct them to land near ... actually, between ... the coordinates she gave me for Jacobs' last known position and the reported location of Taggart's camp. The satellite images show a large open area there that should be big enough for us to treat this like a hot LZ."

A "hot" LZ was a landing zone where hostile contact was not only anticipated, it was expected. The insertion technique for a hot LZ was for the chopper to plummet to within a few feet of the ground and hover there while the troops exited the craft as quickly as possible, ran a few meters past the whirling rotors, and threw themselves down into a prone position in a three-hundred-sixty-degree perimeter. The chopper pilots would only hover for a matter of seconds before shoving the throttles to full combat power and getting the hell out of Dodge. Blue Team and all their equipment would have to be down the loading ramp at the tail end of the bird and prone to avoid the risk of decapitation by the massive rotors. It sounded easier than it was.

CHAPTER SEVENTEEN

Day Three, 0410 hours

Jessica's ankle was throbbing painfully, though she gave no outward sign of it. She could feel the tops of her boots biting into the swollen flesh of her calves, but she was managing despite the load she was carrying.

She and Vicky had decided to arm themselves with the American 180s originally intended for Brad and Ving rather than their own Car-4s when there had been no sign of the trio at the drop zone. They had loaded drum magazines in the weapons and then divvied up the heavy spares between them, placing them in canvas satchels they hung around their necks in order to access them quickly when reloading. Jessica had hesitated for a moment and then slung an M-79 grenade launcher over her shoulder and then fastened a bandolier of 40 mm ammo around her waist.

Vicky's eyebrows rose questioningly. "Do you really think you should try to carry all that with a bum ankle?"

"I can hang, Vicky, and you've got enough to deal with carrying the CIWE bag." Her face bore a stubborn look that told Vicky her younger companion would brook no further argument. They had hurriedly stashed the parachutes and harnesses.

They were both troubled by the team's absence, which was totally out of character for them, but neither woman was willing to quit. Taggart, with his twenty-odd men and his crew-served weapons, represented a hell of a risk to them, but it just wasn't in them to give up on Brad and the others. They refused to even consider the possibility that the three might have been taken captive ... or worse. Vicky felt in her heart that her bond with Brad was so strong that she would feel it like a physical pain if he were gone. He was out there ...

somewhere ... and he needed her and the ordnance they were bringing.

Vicky's eyes opened wide as a thought flashed across her mind. In an instant she had opened the CIWE bag and was rummaging through the contents, feeling blindly for the package containing the earwigs Fly had given them before the mission to El Salvador. They weren't there. She spoke a few very unladylike words.

"What's wrong?"

"I didn't bring the earwigs." The earwigs were capable of allowing them not only to talk to each other but to communicate with Fly as well. The vast mountain range closed in around them and they were surrounded by emptiness and the sound of the wind blowing. The only things they had going for them were the bright moonlit night and the fact that they were armed to the teeth. There was nothing to do but forge ahead. Adapt, improvise, overcome.

"Taggart's camp is that way." Vicky pointed generally northeastward, toward where she and Jessica had seen the campfire lights during their descent. "We need to stick to the trees as much as possible, Jess. You aren't going to be able to move very fast in the open areas with that ankle. That bluff above Taggart's encampment will give us a good view down into Taggart's camp, and we should be able to spot Brad and the guys from there if he's got them."

"Or if they've lost their minds and have decided to take that crowd on with no backup," Jessica muttered. She gritted her teeth. "I'll keep up." They began to move, headed for the closest stand of whitebark pine trees, unknowingly following the same path Brad, Ving, and Jared had taken almost two hours before.

Day Three, 0438 hours

In fifteen or twenty minutes or so, the geographical center of the sun would reach a height of eighteen degrees below the level of the horizon, and BMNT (Begin Morning Nautical Twilight) would enable man to detect silhouettes of trees and mountains against the sky. No shadows would be cast, and the brightness of the moon would diminish somewhat. It was a dangerous time for defenders, and an advantageous time for attackers. Most military units observe BMNT with heightened security by "standing to", a procedure where each individual adopts a defensive posture. This tactic dates back as far as the French and Indian Wars, when warriors on both sides would initiate attacks on their enemies in the hours of nautical dawn.

Jared split off from Brad and Ving more than a hundred meters away from Taggart's camp, heading up the steep scree-covered incline that led to the ridgeline that terminated at the bluff overlooking the camp. It was slow going, and he had to really concentrate to keep from sending a shower of tiny rocks tumbling down the incline and warning anyone within hearing distance that he was coming. Jared Smoot was a legend among special operators, especially in the Corps, because of his innate ability to blend into the scenery and become invisible. Even in his civilian clothes he favored the colors similar to that of faded, washed-out old Marine utilities. Camouflage was fine for others, but Jared favored the faded gray-green because it allowed natural shadow and light to mimic his surroundings and break up the outline of his body, and he became one with his environment.

There were few shrubs and scrub trees on the slope, but he took maximum advantage of every one. It was a slow, laborious procedure, one that he had utilized many times and one that had never failed to achieve the desired result.

As he neared the point where the top of the ridgeline leveled off at the top of the bluff, the scree gave way to soil sparsely covered with grass, and he relaxed a little, moving a little faster, eager to scout out the bluff top for the best shooting position from which to fire down into the camp. He was thinking ahead to that second shot, the one he wanted to put into Taggart's head—and that was nearly his undoing.

He had moved onto his hands and feet in order to move onto the crest when he found himself face-to-face with a man half his age wearing camouflage utilities, name tags and patches torn off but the Anchor and Globe stencil still visible on the breast pocket. Eyes wide with surprise, the young man scrabbled to take the M-16 slung over his shoulder and opened his mouth to scream.

Jared dropped his Sharps to the ground, whipping his razor sharp Kabar from its scabbard and springing forward simultaneously. In a single smooth motion, he grabbed the man's chin in one hand, effectively closing his mouth, spun him around, and plunged the Kabar in just beneath the sternum, angling it upwards into the heart. The younger man was dead before Jared eased him and his rifle to the ground. He felt no satisfaction, only dismay that he had almost permitted himself to get caught and ruin the entire operation ... not to mention the fact that he would probably have gotten Brad, Ving, and Ainsley killed at the same time.

* * *

Brad's elbows and knees were sore from low crawling over the rocky ground, and he had dinged them now and again on loose stones. The clothes he wore for fishing and camping were not as durable as his utilities or nightsuits, and they were now ripped and ragged, exposing the skin on his elbows and knees to abrasion. The skin on his contact points was raw and painful, but he forced the pain from that and the dull ache in his side from his stab wound into a separate compartment in his mind. He needed every shred of his focus on what was now, to all intents and purposes, the mission. A little pain was nothing compared to the loss of his life ... or Ainsley's.

He inched along the stony ground just inside the copse of trees that concealed Taggart's camp from view, stopping frequently to listen. There was little activity within the camp, and the two men he had passed in the LP/OP had been awake but not very alert, just as he'd expected. He was close enough now to hear the slow crackle of the campfires. Three of the smaller fires had gone out completely and were smoldering. The main fire was still burning, but it had been reduced to little more than small flames and brightly glowing embers.

There was one man sitting cross-legged on the ground, his eyes fixed on something in the coals. Brad knew exactly what the man was feeling. The coals in a fire could be hypnotic, especially in the wee hours when you were tired and a little sleepy. Campfires were anathema to warriors. Their warmth made you comfortable and drowsy, the fragrant smoke gave your position away through multiple senses—sight, smell, and sound. In combat, comfort was rarely your friend.

His eyes ranged the camp, avoiding the fires as much as possible so as not to destroy his night vision. The smallest tent, the GP Small, was apart from the others and obviously Taggart's. He could detect no activity there. Surprisingly, no one was manning the crew-served weapons, a fact that would weigh heavily in Brad's favor when Jared took out Ainsley's guard.

Quietly, Brad set small aiming sticks that would enable him to shift from one crew-served position to the other quickly in the near darkness. He cradled his Weatherby and eased the safety off, muffling the sound with a fold of his shirt. Then he settled back to wait for Jared to initiate the P.O.W. snatch.

* * *

Ving was moving so slowly he could swear a snail could pass him like he was backing up. Of the three of them, only Jared could surpass him in his ability to conduct a reconnaissance undetected. On one occasion he had gotten so close to a Taliban fighter sitting around a fire with several others that he could have reached out and touched the man. He could still remember the smell of lamb stew spiced with coriander, onion, and turmeric and the aroma of *nan-e-tawagy* (a coarse flatbread cooked on heated rocks in the field). It wasn't bacon, of course, but he had been really hungry at the time and it *had* smelled tasty.

Can't let my mind wander like that ... gonna get myself killed an' I swear Willona would come after me raisin' forty-seven kinds a hell. Can a dead man get haunted by the livin'? If it's possible, she could damned sure do it... Love for his wife and his sons filled his heart, and the feeling brought a calmness and clarity to him, the focus he needed for this screwed up mission they were on. It wasn't Brad's fault. He'd had no idea that he would witness the abduction of a billionaire out in the wilds of Wyoming, and the odds against any one of the three of them running into Taggart again had been astronomical. Yet here they were, getting ready to pull off a wild-ass P.O.W. snatch.

On a normal mission, especially now that they had Fly and all her high-tech gadgets, they would have had vastly superior firepower, communications, four more warm bodies, and time to prepare. Those things tended to mitigate the odds against them and Ving would have been less concerned about the outcome. As it stood, they had three hunting rifles, one of which was a single shot antique, their wits, and hopefully the element of surprise. There was no doubt in his mind about Jared's ability to take out Ainsley's guard … that guy was a dead man walking and had no idea what was coming.

There would be a loud report from the Sharps when Jared cut loose, but there would probably be an echo from the rock face of the bluff. It would give them a few minutes of confusion before they could get organized, but hopefully Brad would introduce more when he started taking out the crew-served weapons gunners. Jared would keep firing, but that damned Sharps was slow to reload and the man had a limited amount of ammo.

Those moments of chaos were all the time Ving had to race in, snatch the handcuff key from the dead guard, unlock the cuffs, and spirit Ainsley away from the camp. Even if everything went off according to the plan (and ops *never* went off according to plan, it was a law of nature) Ving figured they had a one-in-ten chance of an outcome that didn't involve three dead bodies from Dallas and one from Silicon Valley. Still, it was the only game in town, and none of them were willing to abandon Ainsley to whatever unpleasantness Taggart had in store for him.

Ving's eyes roamed the camp, searching for a better place of concealment even closer to the stake Ainsley was cuffed around. It still wasn't light out, and the firelight, even though he was careful not to look directly at any of the campfires, was playing hell with his night vision. Eventually he noticed a depression large enough for him to crawl into under a fallen log less than a dozen feet from where Ainsley was sitting.

The sitting position he was in looked uncomfortable as hell, with his arms and legs wrapped around the stake, his hands cuffed in front, and his face pressed hard against the rough whitepine bark. The tricky part was going to be getting to the log without the guard seeing him. The guy was ex-military, that much was obvious. He was alert and conscientious, moving his eyes around, scanning his surroundings without looking directly at the fires ... he was taking his job seriously.

Ving crept forward, Remington cradled in his arms, elbows and knees moving forward an inch at a time, freezing in place when the guard's eyes roved over the area where he was lying and inching forward as soon as the man's peripheral vision swept past him. Motion would be far more detectable than Ving's bulky, dark-clothed figure would be. It was a tedious process, and it was agonizingly slow. He made it to the depression with only minutes to spare before BMNT, and the guard made no sign that he had been spotted. All that Ving could do now was watch and wait.

* * *

Vicky's back and arms ached, and her legs felt leaden. She prided herself on her personal fitness, but the CIWE bag, the steep mountain slope, and the thin mountain air on top of the lack of sleep had taken a toll on her. The only thing that was keeping her going was her concern for Brad, Ving, and Jared. Jessica, a few meters behind her, was fighting off the pain in her ankle, which was becoming increasingly hard to bear. Still, she kept walking.

Vicky kept glancing at the luminous dial of her watch, nervously keeping her eye on the time and then gazing up at the horizon. It was already a little after 0500 hours and they were still a few hundred meters from the bluff behind Taggart's camp. There had been no sign of the guys or of Taggart's men. It was as if she and Jessica were the only humans within a hundred miles. *I want to stop and take a breather, but if I let up now I'll never get moving again ... and I doubt Jessica could either. This is not the brightest idea I ever had.* She was immediately ashamed of herself. Wherever Brad was right now, he needed her, and he needed the ordnance she was struggling so mightily to get to him.

The CIWE bag was bad enough, but the American 180 and its large capacity drum magazine weighed in at around twelve pounds, and the spares ran about five pounds each. Along with her rucksack, that added up to a burden she was hard put to carry, much less maintain the kind of stealth needed to approach Taggart's camp. Each step she took was harder than the last.

They came to a stand of trees, beyond which was the final incline leading to the top of the bluff, and Vicky raised a hand for Jessica to halt then beckoned with her index finger for Jess to approach.

"This is it," she whispered. "I hope we can catch a glimpse of Brad and the guys as soon as it gets light enough to see. At the least we can provide them covering fire if and when they start whatever they are planning."

Jessica whispered back, "I don't know, Vicky, this whole deal strikes me as a little cockeyed. We haven't seen any indication that Brad is even here, much less going after Taggart … and what if we screw up whatever they're planning?" She'd had these thoughts earlier, but this was the first time she'd voiced them.

"You've known Brad all your life, Jess. Can you tell me you honestly believe that Brad would leave Ainsley to the tender mercies of somebody like Taggart?"

"Not really."

"I don't either, and I believe he's bold enough to try something foolish like this, even though he hasn't gotten the ordnance he asked Fly for yet. The damned fool is so noble he'd take on impossible odds just because he felt like he was obligated to do so. It's part of his code."

"Yeah Vicky, but you've got to love him for it."

"I love him in spite of it," Vicky muttered. "Come on, let's get this over with."

They moved out, adrenaline pumping energy reserves into their efforts. The scree was treacherous underfoot, and they took great pains not to dislodge the stones. They took the most direct route up the slope, fearful that BMNT would catch them partway up.

Jessica heard Vicky gasp when they neared the top, and she froze while Vicky crouched down low to the ground, her American 180 at the ready position. Jessica flicked off the safety on her own submachine gun and brought the muzzle around to the front. Vicky beckoned her forward, and she moved cautiously and silently to the woman's side. There, on the ground at Vicky's feet, was the body of a young man dressed in cammies, a vast bloodstain spread over his blouse. Vicky reached out and touched the side of his throat, checking for a pulse.

"Not dead long, he's still warm," she murmured. Then she beckoned Jessica to move to the side, and together they crested the bluff, weapons at the ready ... only to find themselves staring down the long barrel of Jared's Sharps rifle.

* * *

"What the hell?" he hissed, taking in the sight of the two women. Vicky opened her mouth to respond, but Jared put his index finger over his lips and pointed out two spots near the lip of the bluff. He extended his hand, palm downward, to indicate that they should low crawl to the spots, then he forked his index and middle fingers and pointed them first at his own eyes then down in the direction of the camp.

Vicky stared at him and then silently mouthed one word. *Brad?*

Jared made a circle of his thumb and index finger, other fingers extended to indicate "okay", and then pointed below.

Bursting with unanswered questions, Vicky and Jessica both crawled to the spots he'd indicated. They had an unimpeded view of the camp, and both women carefully studied the site, marking Ainsley's' location, the three crew-served weapons positions, and the smaller tent set apart from the others at a glance. Vicky searched anxiously for any sign of Brad or Ving, but there was nothing. She glanced over at Jared, who merely nodded and then pointed toward the camp.

CHAPTER EIGHTEEN

Day Three, 0537 hours

Jared signed that they should unass their gear and then crawl backwards away from their positions. They complied, careful not to make a sound. Then they quietly backed away from the precipice and crawled to a spot about twenty feet from the edge.

Jessica opened her mouth to whisper a question, but Jared again put his index finger to his lips and began to murmur. Most people don't realize that a murmur is harder to detect than a whisper, but it is a lesson every combat veteran is well aware of.

"No time to explain. Brad and Ving are in position and the P.O.W. snatch will begin at my signal." He noticed with approval that both women were carrying the 180s and then murmured again. "I will initiate by taking out Ainsley's guard. Brad is going to take out one of the '60 gunners as soon as the guard drops. You two need to focus on the other two crew-served positions and then provide suppressive fire towards the troop tents in the confusion."

Vicky and Jessica nodded their understanding, and then Vicky flashed a look back toward the dead man. Jared nodded and tapped the Kabar on his hip. His meaning was clear.

They took their positions again, keeping their heads low to the ground to ensure that they weren't silhouetted when the sunlight broke the horizon. Then they settled in to wait.

Jared eased the Sharps onto the top of his butt pack, which he had carefully situated to provide a rest from which to shoot. The range was so short that he flipped up the Vernier tang sight and adjusted it to zero minutes of angle before tightening the eye cup back down. He didn't bother with adjusting for windage because both the bluff itself and the copse of trees were blocking most of the wind. There was nothing more to do but wait for the light to get just good enough for good target acquisition, so he laid the rifle down.

The surprise appearance of Vicky and Jessica had filled him with elation, and it had boosted his confidence immeasurably. He was almost pathetically happy to see that they had brought the submachine guns and just as happy to see the M-79 Jessica had slung over her shoulder. The odds against them had just shortened in a major way.

On an impulse, he low crawled over to Jessica and tapped her on the shoulder. With signs, he made her understand that he wanted her to give him the M-79, which she gave him gratefully. He then tapped the bandolier of 40 mm shells, which she quickly relinquished. He crawled back to his position and then carefully removed four rounds and laid them out beside the grenade launcher so that he could load them quickly and easily after he'd fired the first two rounds out of the Sharps.

Ainsley's guard was a priority, but he fully intended to go after Taggart next. That was a debt long overdue and he meant to collect it that very morning.

* * *

Vicky was nervous as hell, barely able to control the trembling in her hands that was not due to fear but tension. She strained her eyes trying to locate Brad or Ving, but they were far too well concealed for that to happen. That should not have surprised her, she was intimately acquainted with their extraordinary combat skills.

Her eyes swept from one side of the camp to the other, constantly moving because she knew that if she tried to focus solely on one thing they would begin to play tricks on her. A quick glance at Ainsley told her that he was not feeling well at all. His leg was badly swollen and so was his jaw. She worried about how they were going to be able to extract him in his condition. From the looks of him, he'd not been able to sleep at all, and that was going to be a hindrance as well. The odds were still stacked against them.

* * *

Jessica was still worried. She had not seen Brad yet, and from the looks of things, they would still need a great deal of luck to pull this off because they were so badly outnumbered. This would have been a lot easier if it had been a regular mission. Sometimes she would get bored by the way Brad insisted on mission prep and the sheer monotony of the endless inspections and rehearsals, but now, because there had been none, she could fully appreciate what they accomplished for her. At the moment, she didn't have a whole lot of confidence in this op at all. It was hard to keep from fidgeting, but she forced herself to do it, gripping the American 180 tightly in her hands.

* * *

Dawn was not far away, the light shining above the horizon was beginning to brighten noticeably. Jared pulled the first of the set triggers back slowly until he felt rather than heard the click of it locking in place. Then he raised the barrel of the Sharps and centered the sight on Ainsley's guard's head. Pursing his lips, he whistled a creditable imitation of a Texas bob-white quail and watched as the guard's head swiveled around to face him. With an instinct born of years of experience, Jared's index finger squeezed the front trigger smoothly, and then the guard was sprawled out on the ground in front of Ainsley.

Time seemed to freeze for all of them, everything happening at once but seemingly in slow motion like one of those old silent movies from the '20s.

Almost immediately after Jared fired the first shot, men began to pour out of the tents. Some raced for the M-60s mounted on their tripods and others scattered. Another shot rang out, this time from the east side of the camp, and the first of the '60 gunners fell across their weapon. Brad had been heard from.

Jared, reloading the Sharps, saw Ving sprint from beneath a fallen log and race over to the dead guard to rifle through his pockets. That confused him for a second until he saw Ving pull a tiny key from the man's pockets and then unlock the handcuffs binding Ainsley to his stake. Movement from the GP Small caught his eye and he saw Taggart dive from the opening to a position behind the half stone wall surrounding it. That happened so fast that Jared could not get off a shot, which enraged him. Frustrated, he dropped the Sharps and picked up the M-79, loading, firing, and reloading as fast as he could. The first three went to the woods on the west side of the camp, causing the confusion and chaos he was going for. The fourth round landed almost directly behind the spot where Taggart had disappeared, but Jared had the sickening feeling in his gut that told him he had failed to get his man.

Vicky and Jessica were at a loss as to which targets to fire on until shots rang out wildly from the woods on the west side of the camp, bouncing of the bluff face and ricocheting off into the sky. They both emptied the drum magazines in six to nine-round bursts into the M-60 emplacements and then fumbled in the canvas satchels they carried for a replacement. Both were petrified because they were afraid of hitting Brad, whom they had not yet seen, but they had no choice. They replaced the heavy drums quickly and shot the bolts before laying down a withering fusillade. The American 180s made a sound like two chainsaws.

Jared tore another few rounds of 40 mm from the bandolier and screamed at them, "Run!" Then he lobbed the grenades into the copse of trees on the west side and raced after them down the incline.

* * *

Ving, impatient to get the hell out of there, decided that the quickest way to get Ainsley out of the camp was going to be to carry him. He'd just slipped the younger man over his shoulder in a fireman's carry when the first grenade from Jared's M-79 went off behind him. "What the hell?" He was confused, but he was too busy running for the trees on the east side of the camp to do more than be grateful for the added distraction. He felt a slap at the back of his muscular thigh but he kept running anyway. All hell was breaking loose around him, but he knew Taggart's men would rally soon and he needed to be as far away as he could get when that happened.

As he was running he saw Brad's head and shoulders pop up from behind another fallen log and Brad raised his right arm, clenching his fist and pumping the air with it, the signal for "Hurry up."

"It ain't like I need any encouragement," he gasped, but he kept running. He glimpsed Brad aiming the big Weatherby and saw the muzzle flash as the .300 Weatherby Magnum round exploded out the end of the barrel. He imagined that he heard a cry of pain an instant later, but he was sure it was his fertile brain working overtime. Whoever was firing that M-79 was really adding to the chaos, that was for sure. The tree line was only twenty yards away.

* * *

Brad saw Ving race out to get Ainsley, and his heart caught in his throat as the big man rifled through the downed guard's pockets for the handcuff key. He had fired a couple of shots at the men fleeing the tents after he had taken out the first '60 gunner when he saw Ainsley stagger and Ving sling him over his shoulder. The chainsaw buzz of the American 180s from the top of the bluff literally shocked him, but when he saw the rounds peppering the top and sides of the two GP Mediums he breathed a sigh of relief. *Where the hell did Jared get those ... and who the hell is firing them?* There wasn't time to figure that one out.

Taggart's men had begun to return fire toward the top of the bluff from the trees across the way, and he could finally get a clear target. They didn't realize he was there yet, their attention was on the top of the bluff. None of them seemed to notice Ving and Ainsley until Ving was almost across the clearing. A man in cammies leveled an M-16 at Ving and Brad popped up from behind his cover and pumped his arm in the signal to run like a bat out of hell. Then he shouldered the Weatherby and fired off a hasty shot at the guy in cammies. It struck home, and Brad began to search for other targets, especially Taggart. He wanted desperately to take that bastard out.

Ving was almost out of the clearing, and Taggart's men seemed to be getting their bearings. Brad stood up and supporting fire immediately began to rain down on Taggart's crew, causing them to back into the woods on the west side. One brave soul ran across perhaps twenty yards of open space and flipped into the middle crew-served position, and seconds later he was firing blindly at the top of the bluff. Brad chose to use it as a diversion, and he ran, bent double, into the tree line behind Ving. Taggart's men were all firing at the top of the bluff now, but it took them a few moments before they realized that none was coming back at them anymore.

* * *

Taggart emerged from his hiding place, bleeding from a surface scratch, the result of that damned 40 mm round. *Where the hell did that come from? Who's out there?* His face was contorted with rage.

"Jeffries!" he screamed.

"He's down, Gunny, an' it don't look like he's gonna get back up." Jones, the former corpsman, was doing his best to stanch the bleeding from Jeffries' chest wound ... wounds; he looked like somebody had fired three or four rounds of double ought buckshot into him at close range. Jones shook his head in frustration. There were at least a half dozen puncture wounds in Jeffries' chest, and there was no way he could stop the bleeding from the bubbling wounds. Jeffries was going to die and there was nothing he could do to stop it.

Taggart never even blinked. "Hackman!"

The former M.P. responded like the ex-Marine he was.

"Here Gunny!" Hackman rose from the crew-served weapons position in the center of the camp, the smoking M-60 off its T&E (Traverse and Elevation) mechanism and cradled in his arms.

"Round up ever'body that's still on their feet and let's git after them bastards," Taggart roared.

"Even the wounded, Gunny?"

"You hard a hearin', Hackman? If they can walk, we take 'em with us." He turned to the corpsman. "Jones, you stay here. Do what ya can for the wounded."

"Gunny, some of these men need a hospital…"

"Do I look like I got a hospital in my pocket, Jones? Do what ya can for 'em. We got shit ta do!" Taggart was almost foaming at the mouth, spittle flying from his lips as he cursed bitterly. "Grab yer shit an' let's go. They're gettin' away!"

* * *

Fairly flying down the scree-covered slope, Jessica stumbled and fell, sliding several feet downslope before coming to rest when her injured ankle caught between two rocks … the only two rocks on the slope, apparently, that were *not* loose. A lightning bolt of pain shot all the way up to her head, bursting into multicolored blossoms of agony.

"Get up," Vicky gasped, bending over to offer a helping hand.

The words "I don't think I can" almost escaped from her lips, but she knew Taggart and his men were coming, and they were going to be furious. Offered the choice between pain and death, Jessica bit down hard on her lower lip and opted for pain. She was not disappointed, but she managed to endure it without screaming. Vicky slipped an arm around her waist without even asking, and together they hobbled on down the slope.

Jared caught up with them before they had gone a dozen steps further and slipped his free arm around Jessica's waist from the other side, and together they dragged her downslope, her good foot touching the ground only every few steps, her injured ankle sticking out behind her.

"We gotta hurry, they're comin' fast," he panted.

They were almost at the bottom of the slope when Ving emerged from the wooded area, Ainsley slung over his massive shoulder like a sack of flour. Perhaps ten seconds later, Brad burst out of the woods behind him. When he glanced up the slope and saw Vicky and Jessica with Jared, he stopped stock-still, his mouth wide open.

"What the—" His words were cut off by a shout from behind him. Dropping to one knee he whirled around and drew the MEUSOC .45 from its holster, the big, empty Weatherby still in his left hand.

Vicky, leaving Jessica with Jared, ran to kneel by his side, submachine gun at the ready.

"Go Vicky! I don't know how in the hell you got here…" He didn't see any of Taggart's men yet, but they were closing fast. He fired two rounds from the .45, hoping to slow their headlong rush a little. "Quick," he said, "gimme the 180 and the spare mags and get the hell out of here!"

"But—"

"No buts, Vicky. I can hold them off with that thing long enough for the rest of you to get to cover. There's a cluster of boulders on the other side of that next patch of woods, Ving and Jared know where it's at. I'll meet you there... *Now go!*"

She knew he was not talking to her as the man she loved but as the head of the team, and his tone left no doubt that she had just received an order he expected her to obey. She handed him the American 180 and lifted the satchel containing the spare drum mags from around her neck. Then she snatched the Weatherby out of his hands and ran back to Jared and Jessica, who were standing next to Ving and Ainsley. She wrapped her free arm around Jessica's waist and screamed for them to get moving.

"Brad said there's a cluster of boulders the other side of this next stand of trees. He'll meet us there." They rushed toward the next grove, some forty yards away, half dragging Jessica. Nobody noticed that Ving was starting to limp or the bloody hole in the back of his pants leg.

* * *

He knew he had only seconds left before Taggart and his men would break the tree line, so he opened up with the submachine gun, spraying the area from which he had heard the voices come with six to nine-round bursts. The lack of professionalism he had seen in the camp had given him a little confidence, but he hadn't factored in the fact that Taggart's men had felt safe in the remote high reaches of the Wind River Range, and they had in fact been relaxing and enjoying a "stand down". They had been lax because of that, and the only people on alert had been the sentry guarding Ainsley and the guy acting as sergeant of the guard. Even the guys in the LP/OP had been half-assed. The sharp commands coming from behind the trees now belied his initial impressions. As best he could tell, Taggart had broken his men down into two teams and were trying to flank him ... not good.

Ripping the drum magazine from the top of the American 180, Brad sprayed the entire woodline once more then turned and fled as fast as he could in the direction Vicky and the others had moved. He hoped he could reach the next stand of trees before Taggart's crew emerged from the trees. It was a footrace.

* * *

The cluster of boulders was defensible, if only for a short time. Ving had taken Jessica's American 180 and was blocking the widest entry point, while Jared was tending Ainsley and Vicky was checking Jessica's hugely swollen ankle.

"You okay, Ving?" Brad wasn't gasping, but he was slightly winded from his all-out sprint.

"Took one in the back of the leg, Brad, but it's through and through ... already stopped bleeding, but it hurts like a bitch," Ving grunted. The high velocity 5.56 round had obviously cauterized the bullet channel during its passage through his flesh, but Brad knew from personal experience that there would be considerable pain and extensive bruising of the surrounding tissue.

"Can you walk on it?"

"Got here, din't I?"

Brad reached out and clapped Ving's muscular shoulder reassuringly. "Just checking."

"Had me some bacon I'd be sittin' pretty right now." There was humor in his voice, but his brown eyes were cold and slitted, scanning the tree line fifty meters away and missing nothing.

Brad grinned and then turned to Vicky, who was ripping Jessica's trouser leg open because she didn't dare try to unlace her boot.

"Why are you here? I specifically told Fly not to let you two come down here!"

"We wormed it out of her, Brad, don't get pissed at her. I'm not stupid, I knew something was up when she left the comm center to drop off your original ordnance request at Duckworth's private hangar. Besides, Jessica figured it out first, and when I caught up with her in the armory, she was already making up a CIWE bag to bring up here. She was coming whether I did or not." Her stubborn frown told him he was wasting his breath. He'd have to take this up with her later.

"I asked for reinforcements, local law enforcement types, or National Guardsmen…"

Vicky's frown deepened. "I don't know if she got us any or not, Brad. I was so fired up I forgot to call her in the Otter. I was too busy trying to contact you on the sat phone, and by the time I gave up, we were over the DZ."

"You *jumped*? Are you nuts?"

"It's not like we haven't done it before, Brad…"

"Jesus Vicky, a *night* jump in the mountains with no way of knowing what's on your DZ … and the crosswinds!" He was shaking his head in disbelief.

"It's done, Brad, forget about it. Tell me about Taggart's men. How many does he really have?" She had heard the gunfire behind her when they'd left Brad at the foot of the incline.

"I couldn't get a count after you three raked the camp from the bluff top. I counted fourteen that I can confirm during the recon, but I'm certain there were more inside the tents." He turned and cocked an ear, listening for sounds of Taggart's crew approaching. "They're bringing along at least one of the '60s, I heard it cut loose when I cleared that first patch of woods at the incline. They can't be far off, they were only about a hundred meters behind me."

As if on cue, Ving lowered himself into a prone firing position and spoke in a stage whisper. "They're comin'. Looks to be about fifteen of 'em, an' they're in a pretty solid assault formation. Got a '60 near point an' looks like Taggart is leadin' 'em in person. Doin' the movement to contact drill, none of 'em exposed for more than a second or two." He paused. "Bad shit comin', Brad. This ain't lookin' too good."

Then the '60 kicked in and all hell broke loose.

CHAPTER NINETEEN

Day Three, 0601 hours

"Raines." He answered the call curtly but with civility. The lighting in the fuselage of the Chinook was dim, and he couldn't read the name on the caller I.D. screen so he had no idea who was calling.

"This is Assistant Deputy Director Striker. You are *mission go*, and that comes straight from the director."

"I understand, sir."

"And Raines, we need to talk when you get back. This whole mission came from outside the chain of command, and we are a little disturbed because of the ... *unorthodox* ... approach used to initiate it. The director is not pleased that we did not follow Bureau procedure on this."

"Yes sir, I understand." There was a distinct click on the other end of the call and Raines was left staring at his cell phone.

"Director?" Matthews asked him. Raines, Matthews, and Walker were huddled on the floor behind the cockpit of the Chinook, the floor shuddering as the massive rotors shook the craft. The loading ramp was down and the crew chief was standing on the ramp, tied in with his safety harness and staring out at the rocky ground beneath them. The smell of fuel wafted past him and into the fuselage, which always made Raines feel a little nauseous.

"*Assistant Deputy Director,*" Raines replied drily.

"Uh-oh, the brass isn't happy about this one…"

"Apparently not, but we are mission go. Apparently the director isn't happy because this all originated outside the chain of command."

"They *are* awful fond of Bureau policies and procedures." Matthews smirked.

"I'm guessing that getting his ass chewed by the chairman of the Senate Committee on the Judiciary after hours is not his favorite pastime."

"I guess not." Matthews glanced down at his chronometer and then spoke into his headset. "What's our E.T.A. on the LZ?"

Calvin Peabody didn't bother to look back over his shoulder. These government types were none too friendly, and the guys with them looked pretty badass. He really wasn't comfortable with all the guns and body armor they were wearing either. He'd been young and wild in Vietnam, and the grunts there were used to flying with weapons cocked and locked … it hadn't seemed like such a big deal back then. These guys *looked* like pros, but he didn't know them.

Calvin's co-pilot, Steve Rydell, a younger man who'd flown Sea Knights for the Coast Guard, looked over at Calvin and rolled his eyes. He wasn't a fan of these Feds either, but the money was more than good, so he'd come along. Then he held up two fingers.

"Two minutes to LZ, Cap'n," Calvin called out over the headset microphone. There was a flurry of activity in the back as the team tightened equipment straps and checked their weapons.

The crew chief in the back turned to face Blue Team and raised his right hand, two fingers up, and then extended his hand palm downward, indicating that the men should not try to stand before the chopper came to a final hover. The giant chopper was nosing down and picking up speed, standard practice in a hot insertion. The rotors bit hard into the air when Calvin flared, and the pitch of the noise they were making got deeper ... and louder ... as the nose lifted. He was signaling for the team to exit, but they were well rehearsed. They were crouched, on their feet, their knees flexed, before the Chinook leveled off. Raines, Matthews, and Walker passed between the two ranks and were the first ones off the ramp. Three long seconds after Calvin had expertly flared to a hover they were all outside and on the ground in prone positions.

Calvin shoved the throttle forward and the bird raced forward in a steep banking climb. Even before the bird was out of earshot, they could hear the distinct sound of an M-60 off to the northwest, even over the howl of the mountain winds. Whoever the gunner was, he was ticking off rounds at the prescribed rate of six to nine-round bursts.

A touch of highly unprofessional annoyance and resentment churned in Raines' gut for just a moment. This mission in unfamiliar terrain, against an uncertain number of hostiles, armed with God knows what, with no time or space to conduct the inspections and rehearsals, and then transporting him in an unfamiliar aircraft to a hot LZ was the antithesis of everything in the HRT training manual. It was his fault ... his debt to Fly Highsmith was intensely personal. It had nothing to do with these men he was leading into harm's way, and there was a very good chance that some of them might pay the ultimate price for *his* failure. Everything in this sequence of events led back to his craving for some stupid candy cigarettes.

"We gotta move, man," Matthews muttered. "That gunfire can't be more than a klick or two from here, and from the sounds of it things are getting hairy."

Fly had told him that Jacobs and his men were only toting sidearms and some hunting rifles, and if that was the case, they were probably getting slaughtered right now. He recognized the sound of the '60, and the M-16s, but there was another sound he was unfamiliar with. He cocked his head to one side and concentrated. It sounded almost like somebody was cutting Christmas trees with a chainsaw. He shrugged his shoulders and then circled his hand above his head and pointed toward the sound of the guns. Blue Team rose quickly to their feet and spread out into two traveling Vee formations, with a single man on point and two flankers. They moved silently, each man periodically glancing at Raines for new hand signals.

The terrain was as difficult as he'd expected it to be, but they were aided by the growing light in the sky. Yet another thing to stick in his craw, they were running later than expected. He could only hope against hope that they weren't too late. He pumped his arm in the "hurry up" signal and they began to move faster. It was bad tactics, but it sounded as if Jacobs and his men were running out of time.

Scott Conrad

* * *

What the hell? That almost sounded like a Chinook! Brad shook his head grimly. He had no time for wishful thinking now. They were pinned down in this cluster of boulders when they should have kept on running, but it was too late to worry about that. He was down to two mags for the .45, one more drum mag for the American 180, and a handful of rounds for the Weatherby. Everybody except Ainsley had found a spot to bring fire to bear on Taggart's men, but they were all in the same boat with ammo. Pretty soon they would be down to throwing rocks or using their Kabars.

He needed to talk to Ainsley, but the man was positively blue from sitting out cuffed to a pole on stony ground that literally radiated cold, obviously exhausted and just as obviously in extreme pain. His leg was swollen so badly that it looked like an overstuffed sausage casing. The man was nearly comatose.

Bullets were ricocheting off the inside of their makeshift defensive position forcing them to hug the ground and limiting their ability to return fire. If it weren't for Vicky's foresight in bringing the American 180s, they would have already lost this fight.

Taggart's team was getting closer, moving slowly and methodically forward. Brad wondered why the man didn't just wait him out. They were completely blocked in, ammo was running low, and there was no place at all for them to go. If the situation were reversed, he would have laid siege to the place. Any rational warrior would do so in order to minimize casualties to his own men ... but then Taggart wasn't rational, was he? The man was a lunatic, motivated by resentment, greed, and an absolute *need* to control everything. Clearly, Taggart wasn't planning on taking them prisoner, not even Ainsley. He was going to try to kill them all—and it looked to Brad as if he was going to succeed.

He noticed Jared, who was dangerously exposed as he fired that antique Sharps, had taken his Kabar from its sheath and laid it on the ground where he could pick it up instantly when his ammo ran out. Brad did the same, and, slowly, so did Ving, Vicky, and Jessica. Not one of them even considered trying to surrender. The word was not even in their vocabulary.

* * *

They were moving faster than they usually would have in this kind of terrain and under these circumstances, but the dark-colored HRT jumpsuits made them nearly invisible and the rattle of gunfire must have masked the insertion and the sounds of their movement. Raines could see muzzle flashes perhaps a hundred meters ahead of them. The point man halted and turned to him, signaling that there were two, maybe three, groups engaged around a cluster of boulders up ahead. Matthews, in the first team's vee formation, rushed to Raines' side and took a knee.

"What's up?"

"Looks like we have two, maybe three, groups of hostiles up around that cluster of boulders. Let's separate the teams and try to flank the whole shooting match."

"Any ideas on which one is Jacobs' group?"

"Looks like to me that the east and west groups are firing on the cluster of boulders. If I had to bet money, I'd say Jacobs and his men are using those boulders for cover. I want to take Walker and Flanders with me and try to reach that cluster. I need you to hold the teams in place here until I find out if there's anybody in that cluster or if the two outside groups are shooting at each other."

"Jesus, Larry, you're the Blue Team leader. For God's sake, send the point team up there to check it out."

Raines knew he was violating a fundamental principle of leadership, but his heart told him that he had gotten the team into this mess and he wasn't going to put any more of them at risk than he absolutely had to.

"Don, you're perfectly qualified to lead this team if something happens to me. Now, I'm going to go check out those boulders. I think Jacobs and his guys are in there and that those two groups are trying to flank him."

"But Larry," Matthews said in a low voice no one else could overhear, "what if you're wrong?"

Raines grinned. "What if I'm right? If I'm wrong I'll hotfoot it back here and we can try to outflank the two groups. This is a firefight and it ain't going to last a hell of a lot longer. If I'm right, and I think I am, Jacobs is pinned in those rocks. I'll pop a green star cluster to signal that I'm okay, Jacobs is there, and you can move the men out around Taggart's teams. When you're in place, send up a red star cluster so I can halt the outbound fire from the boulders."

Matthews still didn't like it, but he knew he'd just received an order and he was a professional. "Good luck, Larry." He turned and signaled the teams to take up a prone three-hundred-and-sixty-degree perimeter while Raines, Flanders, and Walker made their way in a low crouch to the beleaguered defensive position inside the boulders.

* * *

It was Ainsley who alerted them to the intruders. Brad had been focused on Taggart's two teams and conserving his ammunition as best he could. Brad, Ving, Jared, Vicky, and Jessica were arranged in a semicircle facing outward, and every one of them had been needed to hold off the assault.

Ainsley, still groggy and shivering, had begun to slowly come around. He wanted more water, but he was more concerned about the ricochets whirring around inside the rock perimeter. Biting back a scream of pain, he threw himself forward onto his belly to present as low a profile as he could ... only to find himself face-to-face with a man wearing a solid-color jumpsuit with a ballistic vest bearing the letters F.B.I. across the front and a military style helmet. Startled, he yelled at the top of his lungs.

"Hey!"

Brad was the first to spin around, pointing the American 180 at the intruder and barely managing to stop himself from sending a burst into the intruder before he noticed the F.B.I. marked on the guy's vest. The guy held up a hand, palm outward, then raised two fingers and pointed back out the way he had slipped in. Before Brad could respond, two more F.B.I. guys crept in and took up firing positions between Vicky and Jessica. Without waiting for further instructions, they began to engage any of Taggart's men who were foolish enough to reveal their positions.

The noise was still too loud for talking, and Raines had already found out about the ricochets ... the hard way. One of them had struck the trauma plate in the center of his vest and thrown him back against one of the boulders. He dived to the rocky floor and looked at Brad. He held up his hands and showed ten fingers, clenched them and then opened them once more then scribed a circle in the air.

Brad nodded his understanding. *The F.B.I. special HRT unit is here, and he has twenty more men outside ... but where the hell are they?* He didn't have long to wonder. The Fed reached into a pocket on his vest and pulled something out, something Brad recognized instantly. A star cluster, a flare of sorts that sent up different color sets of five 'stars', commonly used in the military as a signal pyrotechnic. It consisted of an aluminum tube about a foot long with a cap of the same material slipped over one end. To use it, you had to slip the cap off and slip it over the other end. Inside the cap was a firing pin. When the firing pin went over the primer, a hard tap on the top of the cap set off the flare ... and that's exactly what the Fed did. Then he began to scream, "Cease fire," and make a cutting motion across his throat.

Ving and all the others except Jared whipped around when the star cluster went up and saw Brad repeating the sawing motion across his throat. They stopped firing, but Jared continued to stare out toward Taggart's men, his Sharps loaded with his last round. He was looking for Taggart.

As soon as the star cluster exploded above, surprised shouts and screams accompanied a massive burst of gunfire. Taggart's men resisted briefly and then were driven backwards into the open, where the rising sun exposed them. Some of them threw down their weapons and raised their hands in surrender.

A howl of rage emanated from the lungs of one man, and he fired at several of the men with their hands up, cutting them down like jackstraws.

"Gotcha, you sonofabitch," Jared muttered then raised the buffalo rifle and leveled his sights on the head of the howler, the first set trigger already cocked.

Raines, recognizing Jared's intent, shouted "Wait," but it was already too late. Jared squeezed the front trigger and Taggart's head exploded in a cloud of blood droplets and bone fragments. The firefight outside their perimeter raged on full force for only a few seconds more before the bulk of Taggart's men surrendered. Sporadic gunfire continued, getting farther and farther away as the HRT mopped up and then continued up to Taggart's camp.

* * *

"'Bout time y'all showed up," Ving drawled. Only seconds before he had been mentally saying goodbye to Willona and his sons, sure that his time had come. Now he felt like a deflated balloon.

"You're welcome," Raines said, getting to his feet and crossing over to Brad, extending a hand to help him up. "Larry Raines."

"Brad Jacobs... Man, am I glad to see you!" He froze then whipped around to check on Ainsley. Vicky was already tending to the multi-billionaire. "He okay?"

"He's going to be fine if we can get him to a doctor, Brad." She uncapped her canteen and held the back of Ainsley's head as she tipped it up to his lips. Ainsley drank as if he was dying of thirst. When he'd had as much as his stomach would take, he leaned back against a boulder and let his eyes range over the group that had saved him from that maniac Taggart and his men.

"Who are you guys?"

"My name is Brad Jacobs, Mr. Ainsley, and these gentlemen are, unless I'm sadly mistaken, members of the F.B.I. Hostage Rescue Team." Brad gestured toward Raines.

"Wow, Taggart must have called Shepard after all…"

"Actually, I called Mr. Shepard. It was his call to Senator Perkins that got this mission approved."

Ainsley looked surprised. "Then how…?"

"Mr. Jacobs here spotted you being chased across the lake from where he was fishing and recognized both you and Taggart. It was his call to an old friend of mine that led to your rescue."

"I don't understand."

Brad spoke up quickly. "That's not important right now, we can talk about it later. Right now we need to get you to a doctor."

"Ving needs one too," Jessica piped up. She was bent over Ving's left leg, placing antibiotic ointment and a field compress over both his entry and exit wounds. She had cut his pants leg off above the knee and swabbed the areas with alcohol pads first.

"I don't need no doctor," Ving drawled, his voice deep and tired sounding. "Jess done fixed me up just fine." Then he grinned, his white teeth glistening brilliantly in the early morning light. "I don't s'pose you guys brought any bacon with ya?"

Jared, running a patch lovingly through the Sharps' barrel, spoke for the first time since he'd aimed at Taggart and eliminated him. "Don't worry, brother, Willona will feed you plenty of bacon when we get back to Dallas."

Ving's face fell. "Yeah, right after she gets through chewin' my ass for lettin' myself get shot again."

Day Three, 0730 hours

Burl Oates rode up to the camp where Nicholas Ainsley was supposed to be waiting for him, leading a string of pack-laden mountain ponies. He had been up in the mountains for the last two days, taking care of a Minnesota tourist who, as it turned out, had been a pretty knowledgeable guy. He had returned to his own spread and had loaded up the ponies and taken the direct route to the camp instead of going by the outpost store first because he'd gotten a late start. He'd never heard about Simon Perry's death. The only thing he'd noticed that was out of the ordinary was Calvin Peabody's big-ass helicopter roaring around in the sky. Funny, he wasn't aware of any big construction jobs in the area, but he supposed Calvin might have been hired to haul some furnace or other heavy freight up to the northwest. Maybe to the ski resort.

He clucked once and dug his heels into Rosemary's flanks (Rosemary being the name of his roan mare) and urged the pack animals on through the creek. He could see the three tents high up on the bank on the far side of the creek. Not a spot he would have chosen, that's for sure. Weird thing was there was no smoke coming from the campfire pit, and he didn't see a soul stirring ... not what he'd expected from an experienced outdoorsman. He sighed. Wouldn't be the first time a tenderfoot had exaggerated his experience and abilities to him.

"Hello the camp!" he boomed. No answer. Something wasn't right. He eased his .30-30 Marlin lever action rifle out of its scabbard and jacked a round into the chamber then climbed down off Rosemary, leaving her reins dragging on the ground. She was well-trained, and he knew she would stay there till hell froze over or she got thirsty. She wouldn't go further than the creek, even if the pack horses tried to drag her.

He approached the tents on foot. "Hello the camp!" It was then that he heard a groan and saw something make a ripple in the canvas top of the smallest of the tents. Byron Ashworth was still alive.

EPILOGUE

Dallas, Texas

"There was no way I was going to stay here, Brad Jacobs!" Vicky was mad as hell. "We had no way of knowing how much trouble you were in, but we had a pretty good idea you were going to jump in over your head." She crossed her arms over her breasts and turned away from him. "It's your own damned fault you know. If you weren't so damned *noble...*"

"Baby, I'm not noble..."

"It's that damned macho code of yours, Brad. It makes you so predictable." She had used the word damned three times in two sentences, which told him she really was angry. When he turned her gently around to face him, he saw that she was crying. That was the one thing on Earth he was not able to handle.

"I'm sorry Vicky, but I can't change that for anybody, not even you."

"Don't be so damned self-effacing, Brad. I love you for what you are, but sometimes it's so hard to adhere to your standards."

There was nothing he could say to that. His code was hard to live up to, but he didn't expect anyone else to understand or even live up to it. It was simply a part of him, forged in the crucible of the Corps and in combat. He could no more change the way he was than he could move the moon and the stars. His code defined him.

Vicky turned her sea-green eyes up to his, and then she broke down and wrapped her arms around his neck.

"I know you're the boss when it comes to Team Dallas, and I know that you give the orders." She kissed him then drew back. "Just don't ever give me an order again that you know I can't follow."

He gave her a wry smile. That was another fundamental rule for leaders. Never give an order you know will not be obeyed. He wrapped one arm over her shoulders, and together they walked out to the corral behind the barn. They could hear the carpenters, plumbers, and electricians pounding away inside the barn under Fly's watchful eye. The sunset over the corral was stunning, and they stood there, quietly watching, as the Texas sky turned into a kaleidoscope of breathtaking colors.

When they finally turned to go back inside, they saw Ving sitting on the back porch of the carriage house that Willona had bought for them when she closed the deal with Duckworth for the ranchette. He had his leg propped up on a stool and an ice-cold Lone Star beer in his hand.

"Y'all come on up and set a spell! Willona an' the boys are fixin' supper. Plenty for ever'body!"

"What's for supper, Ving?" Vicky was amused but not at all sure Willona was in the mood for company. Just as Ving had said up in the Wind River Range, she had given him pure hell for getting himself shot ... at the same time she was mothering him and clucking over his bullet wound. It had been funny to watch.

A giant grin split Ving's dark face, lighting up the twilight. "Bacon! What else?"

*** THE END ***

Thank you for taking the time to read TRACK DOWN WYOMING. If you enjoyed it, please consider telling your friends or posting a [short review](). Word of mouth is an author's best friend and much appreciated. Thank you, Scott Conrad.

EXCLUSIVE SNEAK PEEK: TRACK DOWN THAILAND – BOOK 8

Thirty former members of China's premier Special Forces unit, clad in night camouflage and heavily armed, lay in a three-hundred-sixty-degree circle at their ORP (Objective Rally Point). Every third man carried a great coil of climbing rope with a folding grappling hook attached to one end. They were waiting for the recon team to return with final confirmation as to the disposition of the monks in the monastery.

The monks themselves were of a militant renegade sect that had taken the martial arts at the core of their religion to a level much higher than the rest of their order had, and as a result had been first disciplined, and then shunned by their peers. After losing their financial backing from the order, the renegades took things a bit further and began to hire themselves out to perform services they were uniquely capable of performing. It was a prime example of religion gone bad. Theft, kidnapping, even assassinations were performed quickly, quietly, and most of all, inconspicuously. It was said that even the least skilled of the monks could make a true ninja look like a rank amateur...

A Brad Jacobs Thriller Series by Scott Conrad:

TRACK DOWN AFRICA – BOOK 1
TRACK DOWN ALASKA – BOOK 2
TRACK DOWN AMAZON – BOOK 3
TRACK DOWN IRAQ – BOOK 4
TRACK DOWN BORNEO – BOOK 5
TRACK DOWN EL SALVADOR – BOOK 6
TRACK DOWN WYOMING – BOOK 7
TRACK DOWN THAILAND – BOOK 8

Visit the author at: **ScottConradBooks.com**

Printed in Great Britain
by Amazon